More books by Greg Cornwell

Twilight – A defence of death with dignity

The John Order Series:

Order and the Abandoned Body

Order and the Merimbula Mystery

Order and the Luckless Lovers

Order and the Parliamentary Conference

Order and the Motel Murder

Order and the Curse Crime

JOHN ORDER POLITICIAN & SLEUTH SERIES BOOK 8

GREG CORNWELL

ORDER

AND THE
CURSE CRIME

Copyright © 2020 Greg Cornwell

ISBN: 978-1-925952-93-3
Published by Vivid Publishing
A division of Fontaine Publishing Group
P.O. Box 948, Fremantle
Western Australia 6959
www.vividpublishing.com.au

Cataloguing-in-Publication data is held at the National Library of Australia.

To Meg, as always.

ONE

The single line moved slowly to the desk where passengers' exchanged their passports for the ship's security card and had their photograph taken. It was awkward for some, pushing a carry-on with a foot while they held the passport and a complimentary glass of champagne in their hands.

Emmie – Marilyn Elizabeth, ME, get it? – brunette, medium height, early 40's was ahead of John Order and sipping from her flute when the thick-set man who had moved out of the queue for some reason rudely pushed back in, jolting her without apology.

Order opened his mouth to protest, noting the sharp look perhaps of recognition the man gave him, but checked his words as Emmie gently shook her head. We're sailing together, she seemed to signal, let's not have an early falling out with someone.

Accompanied by a plump pleasant stewardess, their documentation complete, they were led to their cabin, or suite as they now were called, where Emmie expressed delight at the bedroom, sitting room, open balcony, walk-in wardrobe and fully equipped bathroom. Their luggage awaited them and the arrival of their butler, a young Sri Lankan, who opened the free bottle of prosecco, completed her joy.

It was farewelling the butler into the corridor the suite door opposite opened and the rude man from registration emerged and with another searching look at Order took himself back toward Reception.

John Order, Speaker of the ACT Legislative Assembly, now with a comfortable majority in his electorate thanks to diligent representation and careful cultivation of his voters, normally would not have been surprised at such recognition. His high position in the legislature, years of service and yes, an unfortunate involvement with several bodies, both dead and alive, had provided him with some local public notoriety.

That such should have spread to a cruise liner on a two week voyage to Hong Kong however, was a matter of comment.

"I think I've been spotted," he said to Emmie, wrenching the balcony's sliding door open, oddly flattered nevertheless.

"It won't spoil our holiday, will it, John?" Emmie asked apprehensively.

"I don't see why. It's only one person an' for privacy reasons there's no passenger lists anymore, so people can't be identified."

The absence of passenger lists was an inconvenience in trying to place people you had met, but also offered anonymity for the unmarried like Emmie and John Order travelling together. There always was Google, of course, and in his experience people used it so some gossip still got around. And possibly there were other people from Canberra aboard.

"If it gets too bad however, we can always stay here in the suite," Order murmured quietly into Emmie's ear as they enjoyed the sea breeze on the balcony looking out over Sydney Harbour. "The bed looks very comfortable."

The jab was gentle and accompanied by the question: "Who do you think recognised you?"

Order explained and Emmie responded: "Ah, Mr. Rude."

And the christening was complete.

* * *

The ship made its leisurely way up Australia's east coast in good weather stopping at Brisbane and Cairns before transiting Torres Strait and the Arafura Sea and manoeuvring through the numerous islands of Indonesia to the Philippines.

Emmie improved her tan, becoming more desirable day by day in Order's eyes. For his part he risked severe sunburn so kept himself covered during their long baking's on deck and gradually as the voyage progressed overcame his worries about leaving the Parliament in charge of his feisty deputy Wendy Wonder or Wendy the Wonder Woman, WWW or three W's hence VW for short. It was the winter recess after all and most MLA's were away so mischief would wait and the Clerk could be relied upon to curb any independent behaviour of the Deputy Speaker. On a personal note both he and his friend were both out of town, so no point in raising gossip there.

They saw nothing of Mr. Rude, either during the day or at night in various restaurants or at entertainments. Once returning unexpectedly in the morning for a forgotten hat, Order had sympathy for Rose, the Filipino maid who serviced this block of suites, when he saw the chaos of Rude's accommodation through the open door.

A visit to Cebu, its Taoist temple and Fort San Pedro then overnight to Manila, Intramuros and Rizal Park, tried for a Jai Alai game, rode in a jeepney and a practice shopping run for Hong Kong by Emmie.

Order thought the commotion next morning in the corridor was more than should be expected from disembarking passengers, who the night before had placed their colour-coded heavy luggage outside their doors.

Investigation revealed officers in summer dress whites with impressive-looking yellow epaulettes, a bewildered butler and a distraught Filipino maid.

Mr. Rude had disappeared.

His bed remained turned down, pyjamas neatly folded and the evening chocolate still sitting on the pillow. The sliding door to the balcony was closed but not, to a discerning eye with the Asian sun glinting upon it, locked.

With other passengers in adjoining suites Emmie and Order were interviewed without result. There was confusion as to when Rude had disappeared and how.

Had he been out on the town in Manila and not returned? Had he returned and fallen overboard en route to Hong Kong before going to bed?

The first question was quickly cleared up. The ship's security pass which had led to the original rudeness had been checked back on board. The gap was between the return and Rose next morning finding an unoccupied suite when she arrived to tidy.

Eventually everyone was allowed ashore and they spent several days touring and efficiently pillaging the city's shops. It was Emmie's first visit and Order enjoyed indulging her. The only concern was if QANTAS would allow the extra baggage on board their aircraft for return to Australia.

TWO

The winter break over, the Assembly resumed its legislative routine and Speaker Order also his association with his diplomatic friend, who too had been overseas enjoying the European summer. The affair with Emmie continued as well and despite his wish to establish a more permanent basis Emmie insisted upon maintaining the comfortable informal relationship they enjoyed. That Order wanted more surprised even himself, but he decided to be thankful for small mercies …

Emmie's work as a freelance graphic designer was irregular and she spent most of her inactive time reading newspapers looking for part-time jobs.

She was thus better and earlier placed than John Order, swamped at the beginning of the session with the minutia of government, to see the local news report weeks after they returned home.

"It's him!" Emmie declared in an excited phone call.

Liz, Order's middle-aged efficient secretary, knew nothing of Mr. Rude on the cruise and hadn't drawn her boss's attention to the appeal.

Police seek help in murder inquiry asked the headline, which was followed by a full-face photograph of Mr. Rude.

"But this is impossible," Order claimed to his friend the laconic Detective Inspector Gabby Williams, tapping the newspaper below the phone. "Unless he's risen from the dead."

Fortunately the House was not yet sitting so Order could devote some time to Williams and the ever-silent Sergeant Shanks at the visitor's round table in his office.

"You're sure this was the man you saw on the boat, John?" The scepticism in his voice palpable.

"Positive," he replied emphatically, thinking ship, wondering if he was catching the policeman's monosyllabic replies and if he should introduce Emmie as a backup witness.

"He was known as Creighton Wolf on the ship," said Order, remembering the excited discussion at the door of the man's suite.

"So who was he really?"

"Walter Scott. It's in the paper."

Or Creighton Wolf or both, thought Order.

"So why was he murdered?"

"Not sure. Possibly embezzlement."

"That's not life threatening," said Order, thinking of bankers and lawyers.

"Depends who you've embezzled from," Williams replied stoically.

"So he steals money from the wrong people perhaps an' does a runner, then fakes his disappearance," Order conjectured aloud. "But why come back after all the effort an' if your life was in danger?"

"If it's him."

"His passport's either still on the ship or with the Hong Kong police, which would confirm his identity. The manifest will show anyone else from Canberra in case there was someone aboard wanting to kill him." The term hit-man seemed too dramatic.

"Not necessarily from Canberra, John. This is hardly Capone's Chicago."

Wolf's presence on the ship and his disappearance no longer was in question, Order decided, after Gabby Williams had departed to check on the passport and manifest. And he thought he knew how it was done. All he needed was Emmie's confirmation of a couple of details.

"D'you remember on which side of the ship we docked in Manila an' Hong Kong?" he asked her that evening dining at their favourite Italian trattoria.

"We were wharf-side," Emmie said, showing off her newfound nautical knowledge. "We watched the dancers from our balcony when we arrived in Manila and there was a band playing in Hong Kong. Why?"

"Because Wolf could have disembarked from his balcony on the other side of the ship at either port while we were all distracted by the entertainment."

"Jumped overboard into the harbour?"

"No. Slid down strong ropes to a waiting launch. I recall thinking our deck wasn't all that high from the sea, not like those two thousand passengers or more floating hotels. Remember outside the restaurant the sea looked about two foot below the portholes?"

"But it wasn't dark in Manila and we arrived in daylight in Hong Kong."

"We did have a rainstorm as we arrived in Manila, didn't we? Blotted out everything, I think. Maybe he used it as cover."

"I wouldn't forget the storm, but surely someone would have seen him?"

"If they did an' providing they were not from the ship, why care? Just think a crazy European perhaps. I'm sure he went over the side. The balcony door wasn't locked an' I'll bet one of the rails is bent a little from his weight."

"But the rope – " Emmie began, placing her fork on her plate.

"If he doubled it so someone below held both ends then when he got down they pulled one end and the whole lot came down – no evidence!"

"How would he manage without a passport?"

"In any of those teeming Asian ports he'd find another, particularly as he'd obviously arranged matters in advance. But why, after all the preparation, why did he come back?"

"I've no idea, John, but I can see you're taking another unhealthy interest like times before. Leave it to the police."

"Maybe he expected to be arrested upon arrival," Order ruminated. "So jumped."

"John!"

Fortunately the dessert arrived.

THREE

"**P**lausible," muttered Williams when Order explained how Wolf had got off the ship then grudgingly acknowledged the man was whom Order claimed he was. "The Hong Kong police have the passport."

A concession to Order for his help in the original identification the policeman confirmed he had now held a British document in the name of Walter Scott, but Williams was not giving out more information.

"Police business, John," he stated for probably the hundredth time in their long association.

The media provided a few extra points of background. Scott had checked in for three nights at one of the high-rise hotels on Northbourne Avenue, built years before when Canberra underwent a dramatic and expensive super growth. Some were currently converting to units, although it was claimed the demand for these often restricted living spaces also was in excess to need. The technology now called for to drive government and business in the National Capital didn't require anything, far less humans, to go home to anywhere at night.

Someone had leaked Walter Scott had been stabbed to death in his hotel room, although the reported blue and white police tape blocking off the room and briefly the entire floor and police cars downstairs made the site, if not the method, obvious.

Someone too looked up the theft charge and only could find a $30,000 claim had been made by an unknown person.

"Nothing makes sense, Liz," Order fumed, breaking off from their review of his weekly appointment's diary to address his concerns.

"Why would a mature-aged man take off overseas an' assume a false identity for a piddling thirty grand, an amount people might steal from their employer to play poker machines? An' why would he come back even under an assumed name to where he could be recognised an' murdered?"

"Homesick, perhaps?" Liz was not really interested.

Order was preparing a tart rebuke when the thought came to him.

"Unless he came back for something he couldn't take with him?" And worth dying for, he wondered, as Liz impatiently pulled him back to diary duty.

With sittings beginning the next day after the mid-year break Mr. Speaker Order had no time for further conjecture.

Everyone was keen to get on with their parliamentary duties, which meant enthusiastic shouting across the Chamber at opponents. If specific criticisms over the recess were not remembered in detail, the inability to fully answer the attacks through the media at the time had built up a full head of aggrieved steam from all sides.

Order had his work cut out in Question Time restraining his government colleagues from provoking opposition members then calling upon them to be ejected from the Chamber for being 'highly disorderly'.

As Speaker, Order took his job seriously and impartially. His role was not to act as the Government's referee and he tried to avoid any show of bias. It always was hard work but particularly difficult the first week back from a long recess and he was pleased to vacate the Chair to his deputy after the tumultuous session.

And pleased to return to the matter in hand.

He wasn't forgetting his primary duties he convinced himself as he climbed the stairs to his office, but he would have to be careful. His political life had featured too many dead bodies, so his friends and staff had become concerned about what they saw as an unhealthy interest.

If Walter Scott, Mr. Rude, Creighton Wolf, had come back for something he could not have taken with him, Order conjectured resuming his mind-track as he inattentively watched the debate in the Chamber with the sound turned down, what was it?

Someone, a woman perhaps, or an item? And does someone else have whatever Scott came back for?

It seemed the most logical explanation, with the Hong Kong visit simply to smooth the ground for the ultimate disappearance. Thus the financial theft of such a trivial amount could be seed money to prepare the way and, Order realised with a pleasure like fitting in a piece of jigsaw, also explained the brief return to Canberra if not the unexpected death.

Because if the return here was brief it presupposed whomever or whatever was being collected would not take long, would probably be waiting. What had gone wrong?

The House rose at five-thirty. There seemed to be no advanced planning during the recesses for the legislation which subsequently clogged the Parliament at the end of the sessions. Emmie was out with her friend, Ally, to discuss a prospective job so Order had a free evening.

The office of Creighton Wolf and Associates, Order didn't know what this meant but doubted there were any, was in the small business precinct of Deakin, tucked away in the jumble of cul-de-sacs and narrow streets lined with two storey buildings often with *For Rent* signs outside.

Predictably the rooms on the second floor were locked. Order was peering inside at a reception desk when a young woman from one of the IT company offices which it seemed filled the rest of the floor asked if she could help.

"All locked up," Order said unnecessarily.

"Has been for weeks," the young girl said. "Maybe he's gone bust."

Clearly she didn't read the newspapers and Order thought he'd take a chance.

"Hope not, I've business with him."

"Good, Sas needs the money."

"Sas?"

"His receptionist. She's a single mum an' her two jobs barely make ends meet."

"Two must be tough," Order said sympathetically, "with a child."

"Not that she was busy here, but the Newton Tavern made up for it."

"Barmaid," she explained to his silent question. A horn blared impatiently. "There's my lift, must be off."

The Newton Tavern was not in the most desirable of Canberra's suburbs and the surrounding shopping centre did nothing to lift the rundown impression. Several shops were shuttered, others with the exception of the supermarket and a takeaway were looking empty.

Order removed his coat and tie placing them in the boot. These precautions were hardly necessary: most of the tradesmen had gone home and the watering hole was not popular with suits, however the music was louder than he would have liked for a conversation.

Sas was easily identified. Apart from a bearded man, probably the owner, she was the only person serving. A woman running to fat, shapeless and a tired full face which looked like it expected nothing more from life than she had already received.

Order stood at the end of the bar and, waiting to catch her eye, asked for a beer. It was that sort of place.

"You work for Creighton Wolf?" he stated when Sas delivered the middy.

"Did," she said sourly, taking his money. At least she read the newspapers and probably had been interviewed by the police already.

"Business good?" he asked.

"You a cop? The press?"

He had never done this before but Order placed a fifty dollar note on the counter.

"Neither," was all he said.

"Go an' take a seat over there," Sas replied, simultaneously pocketing the money and pointing to a quiet area of the room. "I get a fifteen minute break about now, I'll just tell Joel."

She joined him with what looked like a glass of lemon squash.

"What d'you want?" she asked.

And Order wasn't sure. Any questioning he'd done was some time back, usually in Opposition, at committee meetings or in the annual Estimates, often with prepared briefs.

"What was the nature of Wolf's work?" he asked and realised how stilted it sounded.

"Why d'you want to know?"

"A friend suggested I get in touch – about money," Order hazarded. "Your boss was in finance?"

"You could say that, although you're the first customer I've ever seen."

"Howso?"

"His business was all done by phone an' only about three clients too."

"So what did you do?"

"Answered the phone, of course. I suppose he wanted a receptionist so he could sound important."

"Computer?"

"No. Look, what are you really on about?" Her suspicions increasing with his questioning. "Who's your friend? Harris Andrew? Phil Newman, perhaps?"

"I can't say," Order defended, realising where the conversation was not leading and cut out.

"That's no surprise," Sas said scornfully, rising. "I've got to get back to work."

In his car heading home Order realised Wolf possibly was involved in a money laundering operation for a few big players and carefully limited any evidence. Not having a computer was a giveaway because although he was IT illiterate he knew hard drives and discs and suchlike were a mine of information to experts.

Sas probably knew more than she let on but he wouldn't be getting anything further from her. She was now too suspicious, however she had provided two interesting names, if only he knew what to do about them.

He began to feel ridiculous. Here he was Speaker of the ACT Legislative Assembly acting like some fictional private detective, offering fifty dollar inducements to talk, collecting names he'd never heard of having dealings with a man who might, probably was, involved in something illegal. A man, he reminded himself, who was dead, murdered, and whom he didn't even like.

What evidence could be presented to Gabby Williams to further the police investigation? What excuse could he make to Emmie or Liz for chasing the matter?

Yet he didn't want to give up the inquiry and not because Creighton Wolf, Mr. Rude, was dead, but for what many would think was a trivial reason: why had the man changed his identity and returned to Canberra?

Order's position in the Assembly removed him from the day-to-day activities of politics and even old friendships suffered because he needed to be aloof. Rob Glasson, now Government Whip, was one such casualty. If Order wished to see him it was on a formal basis not in the openness of the House dining room.

"Who is Harris Andrew?" Order asked his friend over coffee in his office.

"Head of a big construction company – an' subject to a committee inquiry. Why?"

"Name came up recently in conversation, Rob. To do with money." Order didn't go further. "Why the inquiry?"

"You said it: money. Seems the previous government got caught up in a building development worth a tidy bit."

"Howso?"

"You may not remember with your parliamentary duties and old Speaker Chamber's demands but Paddles Porter, our unlamented ex-Chief Minister, agreed to a suggestion by Andrew to add an extra storey to his big development in Kowen. In about three buildings I believe for our increasing needy. It's still half built so we've inherited it, of course."

"I don't follow."

"Patience." Glasson grinned at his friend. "I haven't finished. Being a welfare project government funds were involved but it seems the extra storeys on the completed buildings cost more and were not up to standard. It looked like money had been siphoned off. Hence the inquiry."

And hence Creighton Wolf's money laundering.

"Not that anything will come of it," Glasson continued. "Our Opposition can argue they knew nothing about the rip-off, Andrew will claim increased costs and we will go along with it."

"Andrew's too big to challenge?" Order asked to a rising anger.

"Exactly. Developments all over Canberra an' he keeps a heavy foot in both political camps."

FOUR

The police had finished with the murder site, Order saw, as he sat in heavy traffic on Northbourne Avenue outside the hotel and beside the hideously expensive tram line which ran down the old median strip and had so divided the local community when constructed years before.

Its government proponents had long gone, leaving their successors to deal with the continuing problems, not least the ongoing costs. Rather like the Harris Andrew Kowen development, without the money laundering, of course.

Wednesday was Private Members business, when any backbencher could put forward a motion or legislation for debate if they could get the matter on the Daily Program – no easy task.

The debates always were adjourned and if not reintroduced for discussion within three months the item lapsed. This sensible procedure prevented the Notice Paper, the omnibus collection of everything coming forward, from being unnecessarily cluttered, because as every politician knew so much of what was put up was for immediate publicity.

In the unlikely event what was being proposed ever did come back, its chances of passing was zero. Private Members day was a parliamentary indulgence.

Order now pleased himself whether or not he attended Party room meetings. Very conscious of the speakership's need for impartiality he tried to avoid discussions on tactics, knowing if something unexpected arose, perhaps a suspension of Standing Orders for an important ministerial announcement, the Leader of the House would alert him.

Listening to a backbencher outlining the case for support for her motion on child restraints in public playgrounds irrespective of cost, Order was reminded of his thoughts on money while stuck in the traffic snarl on Northbourne Avenue.

"How's the Kowen inquiry going?" he softly asked Rob Glasson as an argument arose around them.

"Suspended for a time. Perhaps indefinitely. Because of the death."

"Whose?" Couldn't be Wolf's. Order was mystified.

"Andrew's wife. Tell you later." Someone wanted a show of hands the motion should be withdrawn.

Harris Andrew's wife, Grace, had died from a fall downstairs in their two storey penthouse overlooking Lake Burley Griffin at West Basin. Another contentious infill building development of years before.

"Rumour has it she'd been drinking an' slipped," Glasson continued as they walked toward Order's office, the meeting over. "Out of respect for Andrew the committee postponed hearings. Now it's become complicated because Andrew's going overseas."

"An' can't appear."

"Exactly."

"Convenient," Order said as they reached his door.

"Don't read too much into the death, John. Apparently she drank a lot. So much so Harris Andrew stopped taking her to functions."

Unhappy, frustrated, Order wondered. "Did he have a mistress perhaps?" he asked.

"Very discrete if so," Glasson responded.

"How old?"

"Grace? Funeral notice said late fifties, early sixties, as I recall. Harris is no spring chicken either."

"An' when was all this?"

"A couple of weeks after your man, Wolf, wasn't it?"

No reason I should have picked it up, Order silently excused himself as the bells began to summon Members to the Chamber. I didn't know of the Andrew's existence before Sas and they were not in my electorate, so no sympathy card which was mandatory now with Liz.

Order was not selfish. He appreciated his position required Chamber attendance as much as possible. Although he left some of the boring sessions to the deputies he did his share. This was why he missed the phone call.

"Phil Newman," he read from the message slip. "Did he say what he wanted?"

"Only that he wished to speak with you, Mr. Speaker," Beryl advised. "I asked but he wasn't forthcoming."

In the Andrew developments he had forgotten Wolf's other client mentioned by his receptionist.

"Mr. Newman? John Order."

"Thank you for returning my call. You are the John Order on *Ocean Splendour* last month to Hong Kong? If so I'd like to meet with you."

Sitting in his office later in the afternoon following Question Time, Phil Newman proved to be a tall thickset man with a shaven head. He was dressed in a well-cut blue suit, white shirt and, fashionably for years, no tie.

Newman had a slight accent, explaining he was originally German and Neumann, leaving Order to wonder if anyone in this bizarre mystery held their original names.

"I'm not sure I saw you on board, Mr. Order," the man explained. "I'm not a good sailor and I spent most of my time in my cabin in the rough seas."

Order agreed he hadn't seen the man either and waited patiently to learn what this odd reunion was about.

"I believe you met Creighton Wolf?" Newman asked.

"Saw not met," Order corrected.

"So you didn't speak with him? Not at dinner – open seating? Not at functions where the passengers mix?" Newman sounded incredulous.

"No. Not even around the pool or at the buffet lunches. He just didn't seem to be around."

"In his cabin perhaps?"

"Perhaps." More likely on his balcony, Order guessed.

"Then he disappeared. No ideas about that?"

And turned up here again with a false identity, but Order simply denied having an opinion.

"My apologies then for wasting your time, Mr. Order. I thought you spoke with him." Newman rose from his seat.

"You were one of his clients?" Order asked, forestalling his guest's departure.

"Very briefly. Financial negotiations. I'm in property sales."

"D'you know Harris Andrew?"

"By name, of course, but my business is elsewhere."

"Anyone I'd know?"

"No, no, Mr. Order. Commercial in confidence, please." Newman held out his hand. "Thank you again for seeing me."

Order asked Emmie en route to a Scout function that evening in her recollection what the weather had been like on the cruise.

"No rough weather at all. In fact I can tell you now, John, I was a bit scared as I'm not a good sailor. Why d'you ask?"

Risking her wrath, though explaining he hadn't initiated Newman's visit, he told her of the man's excuse for not being sociable.

"You wonder why people waste their money if they're not going to enjoy themselves," Emmie said dismissively, leaving Order with three more questions: was Newman on the cruise at all, why was he curious about Wolf and finally, how did he know Order was sailing on *Ocean Splendour*?

As they took their seats for The Gang Show Order realised the third question could easily be answered. Emmie had been excited about the holiday and probably innocently talked about it to friends. Ally for example. More to the point as the music for the evening began, why was Order's presence on board the ship important?

Order had recourse once again to Rob Glasson, who before his elevation to Government Whip in Opposition had been a member of the Business Liaison taskforce.

"Phil Newman? Another local mover and shaker. I've met him once or twice. Plays his cards close. Property as I recall."

"No gossip?"

"Nothing juicy, if that's what you mean. A lot of these people keep a low profile, their work's contentious."

This Order understood.

For years Canberra had been divided by those who wanted the Bush Capital reputation maintained in fact as well as in theory and the progressives who thought the national seat of government should be high-rise and high maintenance. Inevitably the latter called for property developers to replace, read destroy in the critics' view, much of the older city and suburbs, courting unpopularity.

"I don't think he's married," Glasson added.

Which was more than could be said for Order's diplomatic friend, who contacted him for the obvious reasons of privacy by his seldom used mobile phone.

The discretion shown was no easy task, their clandestine meetings extremely passionate for the limited opportunities, however now further complicated by Order's growing attachment to Emmie.

Order didn't want to admit it but he was growing tired of the game and nervous of its repercussions upon his political position. Particularly as the association involved a middle-ranking diplomat's wife. Why the man hadn't been transferred elsewhere by now was a puzzle, tours usually lasted only a few years and what Order had welcomed as a brief even exotic fling looked increasingly dangerous to both parties.

They met at formal functions: national day celebrations, receptions for visiting dignitaries, musical evenings, once at a dinner party, and often with their partners. A polite exchange of greetings, perhaps a slightly stronger smile which often presaged another tryst at Order's home unit within days …

Such a meeting occurred that evening at the Croatian Embassy. After the courtesy greetings from the Ambassador at the entrance Order with Emmie alongside was drawn to his diplomatic friend, who touched her husband's arm when she recognised him. The man they were talking with also turned: Phil Newman.

FIVE

"So what did you think of Phil Newman?" Order asked as she drove carefully from the suburb of O'Malley. The police breathalyser units usually left the diplomatic functions alone, nobody drank much anyway, but without the blue DC numberplate you shouldn't take a risk.

"He was pleasant enough," Emmie allowed, kicking off her shoes. They were heading for Order's unit in a once controversial development in Yarralumla for coffee and where Emmie now was leaving a few clothes. Casual items. Nevertheless …

"He definitely was not on the cruise," she declared adamantly. "Two can play sleuth, Mr. Detective. I questioned him while we talked and he knew nothing about the boat."

Ship, thought Order, but a second question had been answered.

"He's very friendly with your friends," Emmie continued. "Sees a lot of them."

"Friendship over leasing some property, I'm told, an' now he plays golf with the husband." The 18-hole duration a convenience on several occasions, Order recalled.

As the Assembly moved into high gear for the last parliamentary session of the year Order's time increasingly was occupied with the day to day running of the House, of visiting dignitaries and of a space problem in the committee area, fortunately in a separate building to the parliament itself. He had no time to concern himself with the Wolf-Scott business.

Emmie too was busy. Her freelance graphic design work had picked up to the extent she had rented premises in Woden instead of working from her cluttered flat and was considering employing an assistant.

Order continued his social representations on behalf of the Government. It was well-known the wife of the Chief Minister, Phillip Keane, was not an outgoing person, a circumstance which originally caused malicious gossip when The Chief, as he was known, began turning up to functions with one of his staffers. Now Keane attended major events alone and left the general socialising to Mr. Speaker and his girlfriend.

Emmie enjoyed these activities. Attractive and well-dressed she was becoming as welcome as Order himself and was intelligent enough to realise the exposure did her fledging business no harm. She also delighted in the occasional photograph in the social pages of newspapers and magazines.

The Helping Hand Ball and Auction was one of Canberra's major black tie events raising money for the city's poor. Although Order wondered where all the funds raised were spent by this and the many other charities operating in the affluent National Capital, he could not afford not to attend.

"I thought they'd use it," Emmie said, folding the newspaper so the photographs could be seen. Two smiling couples and, in the next panel, the winner of the top auction prize of dinner with The Chief, a serious Harris Andrew.

Aside from the propriety of Phillip Keane breaking bread with someone under scrutiny by an Assembly committee, Order's attention was drawn to Andrew's beaming tuxedo-clad colleague, Phil Newman.

I didn't think they knew each other, Order recollected, as Emmie cut their own picture for her brag book.

Of course they could have met after his conversation with Newman some time ago, but even this most likely of explanations was challenged at the Property Council lunch a week later.

Everybody interested in building something more expensive and higher than a brick outhouse according to Rob Glasson and all those substantially involved in ACT properties were present.

As the Chief Minister was speaking it was mandatory senior government politicians attend. There were enough guests milling around the foyer and the table seating lists for Order to seek out someone he knew and on the spur of the moment he approached Phil Newman.

"Enjoy the Helping Hand ball?" he asked, appropriately shaking hands.

"Cost me," Newman replied ruefully, "but yes."

"I didn't know you knew Harris Andrew," Order said, deciding he might as well clear up any accidental misunderstanding.

"Handled a few property transactions," Newman said, adding: "And here's the man himself."

Harris Andrew betrayed his background. Thickset, big boned, in his sixties perhaps, he looked uncomfortable in his stripped suit and matching tie loosely knotted. His hands too were big and suggested a lifetime of manual labour.

If uncomfortable at meeting the Speaker of a legislature investigating his operations he greeted Order cordially enough.

"Phil Newman tells me he's handled a few property transactions for you," Order began, determined to avoid construction and development topics.

"For my late wife actually," Andrew offered, a somewhat hoarse voice perhaps from shouting on many building sites.

Order only had time to extend condolences, accepted with a grunt, before guests were asked to move into the dining room and take their seats.

"I hope I'm not wasting your time, Gabby," Order said to the policeman next morning over tea in his office, "but a few matters don't stack up over the Wolf murder."

"It's our job, John," Williams said patiently.

"Of course, an' I'm sure inquiries are continuing, but not every-one's telling the truth."

He explained Newman's lie about being on the cruise, an obvious excuse to find out if Wolf had spoken to him aboard. Newman's denial he had known Andrew when he had had business dealings with him, or at least his wife, and clearly before her death which was well before any recent acquaintanceship. Even Andrew's abrupt reaction to his condolences over her death, while it could have been embarrassment, had seemed to Order more like dismissal.

"So?" asked Gabby Williams irritatingly.

Now Order was embarrassed and in the silence which followed the policeman delivered a short homily.

"Not everybody tells the truth, John, and I should know. But lies don't always suggest crime."

"So what do these lies mean?"

"I've no idea," Gabby said rising and then, perhaps feeling sym-pathetic to his old acquaintance: "Newman was friends with the Andrews or at least Andrew's wife. And no," he said, reacting to Order's wide-eyed question, "no hanky panky."

"Then why lie?"

"No idea. Perhaps embarrassment because the friendship was so close. Newman was not in the house when Mrs Andrew's slipped, by the way."

"So you're investigating?"

"No longer, John. It was an accident. Now I must be off."

* * *

Creighton Wolf aka Walter Scott was dead, murdered, Grace Andrew dead by accident.

With no direct link why was he fretting, Order wondered? Phil Newman did have a tenuous connection with both but then so did Harris Andrew and less tenuous concerning his wife.

As a prominent Canberra business identity Order was sure Andrew would have some history, perhaps even Newman and Wolf. He checked each out privately upon his computer, knowing this way he would not be criticised by staff and friends.

And drew blanks.

The Australian Capital Territory, Canberra, was blessed with the National Library of Australia, a treasure trove of information sitting in the huge columned building beside Lake Burley Griffin. By law virtually every newspaper and every book published in the country was recorded or stored in its impressive bulk. The problem usually was where to begin.

Order was helped by Andrew's unusual first name, nevertheless working back to early Canberra's social activities was not successful. Harris had not achieved status overnight so didn't feature in the National Capital's prominent citizens.

He wondered if the Assembly committee scrutinizing Andrew's development operations could throw some light upon his background. It was a long shot and Order was not surprised when Bettina, the committee secretary, apologetically explained they did not have such information, which in any event was beyond the inquiry's Terms of Reference.

However if it helped, Mr. Speaker, Bettina had some personal background she thought it would be permissible to share.

Order spoke with Bettina in his office one afternoon when the House and the committee – still stalled from speaking with Andrew – was not sitting.

"I'd appreciate my name being kept out of this, Mr. Speaker, because I don't want my mother to get into trouble, but she was so outraged at the neglect of this poor woman she had to confide in someone and it was me."

Bettina's mother worked in a local and upmarket nursing home as a carer, visiting mobile residents and bedridden patients because it catered for both. One of the occupants was a very elderly Agnes Wilde.

"Mum said she was close to ninety and came from Sydney. A widow, she had been brought here by her daughter, Grace Andrew."

"You're sure?" Perhaps it was the break he needed, silently thanking Canberra still was the size where such things could happen.

"Positive. Mum made it her business to find out Mrs. Wilde's background because she was so angry nobody ever visited. The poor old thing had just been dumped there."

Elder abuse, which Order supposed this was in a mild form, was not uncommon, as he knew by experience. He wondered how many lonely old people were rotting away, forgotten save for the monthly payments of their upkeep.

"Can I visit?"

"Sadly no, Mr. Speaker. She died last year. Winter, I think. An appropriate time."

"An' your mother never found out why she was abandoned?"

"Never. But then she didn't speak. Lost her memory perhaps. She was always welcoming with a smile, Mum said, and had a peculiar behaviour. She would point to her throat and say Plumber."

"Plumber?"

"Plumber. At first Mum thought there was something wrong with her digestion which needed attention, but the nursing staff assured her Mrs. Wilde was healthy in that area although they too had noticed the strange behaviour."

Thanking Bettina and assuring her again of his confidence, Order repaired later again to the National Library's newspaper collection, explaining to Emmie he would collect her for a late meal.

The death notice for July the previous year was brief and to the point.

Born in 1940, Order read, married to Arthur Wilde (dec), beloved mother of Grace. Privately cremated.

Order was so pleased he had moved further in what he had come to see was a circle of privacy he almost cancelled dinner with Emmie to continue his investigations.

SIX

He was fortunate Emmie was so preoccupied with establishing her own graphic design company and training Charlotte, recently arrived from Wagga Wagga, in the ways of Canberra and the business. These days she barely had time to accompany him to functions so his trips to the National Library went unremarked, as secret as his continuing liaison with the diplomat's wife.

Order found the newspaper search frustrating. Granted 1940 was wartime and paper restrictions had cut *The Sydney Morning Herald*, the principle source of the city's births, deaths and marriages announcements, down substantially. Maybe in those days people did not declare such events, money was tight with so many young men away fighting and he could find no record of Agnes Wilde's birth, whatever her surname had been.

One death notice however, prominent for those stringent times, raised an intriguing question.

In September 1940 Sir George Plummer (not Plumber), a wealthy shipowner, had died aged 80 at his Point Piper mansion.

Paper shortage or not Order was sure such a notable Sydney citizen would warrant an obituary and abandoning Agnes for a time he sought – successfully – to find one.

Sir George had had a distinguished career. Impoverished background in England, ran away to sea, jumped ship in the colonies and built, unexplained how, a shipping empire. One item stood out:

a comment about the theft in 1925 of the Plummer necklace from the residence.

The press report of the time was brief and, as it turned out, warranted because the story contained farce and brazen behaviour and was suppressed. Only at the trial were the full details revealed and became the subject of an unsurprising monogram of which the National Library had a copy.

Times were tough in 1920's Sydney. The Great War had stripped the country of much of its riches to feed the inexhaustible butchery. Men who returned from the Front, often broken in one way or another, could not find work. Everyone was scrambling to get back to peacetime living and trying to put shattered lives together again.

Crime was widespread and not only among some ex-servicemen. Those lucky enough to have escaped the war found themselves unable to find jobs, which understandably went to veterans.

Living in the teeming dirty dockside streets and hovels of Pyrmont was an unemployed darkhaired attractive 19 year old girl, Grace Dempsey, Order read with sudden interest. The headstrong independent lass soon caught the eye of Tom Wilde, the appropriately named son of a disabled ex-soldier living nearby.

At this point John Order sought writing paper from the desk.

Tom Wilde soon found honest casual work even when available insufficient return for his tastes and with a small group of like-minded young men moved across to the more lucrative activities of theft, principally from the wharves.

No great reader himself, Grace provided the stimulus for a most ambitious scheme: stealing the Plummer necklace, which Grace pointed out in awe from the society pages of *The Sydney Morning Herald*, a copy of which she had picked up in a pub.

Worth an estimated fifty thousand pounds Australian, the owner of this small fortune was the wife of the wealthy shipowner Sir George Plummer, residing at Point Piper, from where Tom Wilde resolved to rob her.

According to the monogram's author, the theft from such a well-known society figure would have immediate repercussions, Tom Wilde realised, and he would need somewhere to hide the necklace until the fuss died down. Yet in spite of such forethought his approach to the actual robbery was remarkably casual – and paid off!

The court report detailed how Tom and a colleague, Albert Jones, in broad daylight entered through the unlocked main gate the grounds of the Plummer mansion and inexplicably made their way through the gardens rather than up the driveway to the house.

This behaviour the housekeeper observing them through a window thought suspicious and called the police. The butler meanwhile presented with two reasonably dressed men took them for semi-professional tradesmen and admitted them. Oddly only then did they cover their faces.

In the entrance hall the thieves had a stroke of luck. Awaiting her mother to go shopping was Harriet Drummond and a nanny nursing in her arms the baby daughter, Prudence.

Wilde, a tough fellow of average height, seized his chance and the baby, simultaneously demanding the necklace.

It was no contest, claimed the monogram author. Harriet in hysterics, the nanny and staff transfixed in shock and fear and Lady Plummer half-way down the staircase from her dressing room. Perhaps only the housekeeper wondered where the police had got to.

For their part the police were sceptical.

There wasn't much attention needed to the 'nobs' far over at Point Piper from their nearest station in the rough docklands and mean streets of Woolloomooloo. A couple of men walking through the Plummer's gardens was trivial to the daily assaults and murders they encountered.

Being the Plummer's they needed to respond, but the police didn't hurry. Probably a couple of drunks who had lost their way. So valuable time was sacrificed while the necklace was produced, baby Prudence a hostage in Tom Wilde's strong arms.

Still the thieves showed enterprise keeping the baby, now crying lustily, with them as they retreated down the driveway to the gate. Here Wilde carefully placed Prudence on the grass in full view of the household who had followed at a safe distance and slipped into the street.

The police, subsequently the laughing stock of Sydney, turned up a few minutes later and realised something was amiss from the commotion inside the property and the behaviour of Albert Jones who, in an involuntary reaction to coppers, began to run.

But neither Wilde nor Jones had the Plummer necklace.

At the trial there was rumour of a third man but nothing was ever proven and neither of the accused revealed such an identity, possibly aware of the fortune awaiting them when released from prison still relatively young men.

Their guilt beyond question Wilde received fifteen years as the ringleader and Albert Jones, his none-too-bright accomplice, ten years. The sentences were mitigated by the lack of violence and the gentle treatment of baby Prudence.

In a postscript the monogram's author advised Jones died in Callan Park Mental Hospital before his sentence expired. Wilde was released in 1941, fathered a child and was called up for military service. He was killed in 1943 in New Guinea when a United States Liberator bomber crashed on take-off into Australian troops deploying from trucks.

The Plummer necklace remained lost.

* * *

Order realised the postscript provided another avenue for re-searching names and after a fruitless 1942 search was rewarded by moving back a year. Here Grace Wilde had given birth to a son, Arthur, perhaps recorded in celebration of her husband's release from prison.

Gabby William's expression read this-had-better-be-good and had not altered when Order explained his theory over tea in the office.

"It's all conjecture, John. An' what's this missing necklace got to do with Creighton Wolf's murder?"

"They're connected, I'm sure. I think Mr. Rude – Wolf – came back to steal it."

"If it's here."

"Evidence points that way. I know it's not conclusive but we have the name Grace running through the family, there's the connection between Grace Wilde, Arthur Wilde, her son's wife Agnes an' Agnes' daughter, Grace again."

"Possible connection," Gabby said unconvincingly.

"Then there's old Agnes' strange behaviour. Pointing to her neck an' saying Plummer."

Williams was silent.

"I think they all know or knew about the necklace and its where-abouts. The secret has been passed down generation to generation but nobody's talking."

"Perhaps there's nothing to talk about?"

"I think there is, but what can we do about it?"

"*We* can do nothing, John. You personally and me as a policeman. A murder has been committed I'm charged with investigating but trying to link it with what, a century old theft, is going too far." Williams' rose to his feet, his expression none too friendly, his tone exasperated. "I'll see myself out."

Inadvertently Order had alerted himself to another possible avenue of pursuit during the unsatisfactory exchange with Gabby: were there more generations of the Wilde family?

Grace Andrew's recent death notice provided Laura, a daughter.

Now came the difficult part. He couldn't approach Harris Andrew for Laura's address without revealing the reason, in which case he might as well ask him direct. He could hardly approach Laura either, why should she talk to him, a stranger?

For the first time Order questioned whether or not the necklace was an obsession getting out of hand.

SEVEN

A part from a surreptitious telephone call to the Andrew penthouse to be told by a foreign domestic Miss Laura didn't live there anymore, Order's attempt to solve the disappearance of the Plummer necklace stalled.

The inaction coincided with a political headache. A Government backbencher was arrested and charged with drink driving following what obviously was a long lunch because it occurred early in the evening.

It really was a matter for Rob Glasson, Government Whip, but several women MLA's from both sides of the Parliament and long-term critics of the licenced House dining room called for its closure. That it only was open at set hours and probably served less alcohol than most bars in the city, any more than the incident must have occurred at a local restaurant for the same reasons, made no difference to their demands.

It became a local issue with the media expanding the story into a list of supposed politician's perks: free newspapers and car parking spaces, subsidized meals and, as always, lavish expense accounts.

Except for the expense payments the other listed benefits fell within Mr. Speaker's area of responsibility and Order on advice from the Assembly Clerk was busy clarifying the existing entitlements and denying the more extravagant claims. No time for the missing necklace.

The issue soon became yesterday's news with a school shooting in Melbourne and another sporting star up on a rape charge. These events coincided with an Assembly non-sitting week so Order could return to the necklace hunt.

The activity in no way resulted in him neglecting his parliamentary duties. In spite of the volume of paper coming into the office and the demands of constituents and Members, Liz and Beryl, Speaker Chamber's former secretary, were running a smooth uncomplicated operation.

Liz efficiently culled the reading matter and handled elector's representations while Beryl, initially so cautious about telephone inquiries for fear of offending someone, had become so adept at dealing with callers she was approached with care by those in regular contact with the office.

Order was unsure of his next move. There was nobody he could use as a conduit to Laura without he believed, for Gabby's response still stung, making a fool of himself.

Non-sitting week or not the social commitments continued and he found himself, unaccompanied this time, at a reception for the launch of a new vehicle showroom in industrial Fyshwick. It was no great surprise to see Phil Newman among the guests and looking as about involved as Order himself.

It was a sudden decision to join the property man and after the obligatory handshake and pleasantries, another decision to ask about Laura.

"I thought you might know her," he explained. "Her background. Where she lives? You're a friend of Harris Andrew."

"Acquaintance," Newman corrected, looking keenly at Order. "Why d'you want to know?"

Here was a problem. He didn't want to be telling strangers, even acquaintances of the Andrew's, of the necklace mystery.

"Somebody said she was a lawyer," he lied, "an' Emmie wants one to set up a company. Emmie is a bit of a feminist an' prefers to deal with women."

"Well she's not. Works at the ANU an' lives in one of the high-rise in Lyneham on Northbourne Avenue. She's in the phone book under L.R." Newman added helpfully.

"No use to Emmie then."

"No, Mr. Order, no use at all," the man said pointedly, leaving no doubt as to his interpretation of the questioning.

Order was sufficiently embarrassed he excused himself and with a quick thank you to the host left the function. Ahead he saw Newman getting into his distinctive PIN number-plated car, mobile to his ear.

Order met Laura the next day over lunch in a coffee shop in Civic just off the Australian National University campus.

A tall plain girl, probably with her mother's features, glasses and a studious expression, late twenties or early thirties perhaps, she wasted no time getting to the point.

"Phil Newman said you wanted to see me," she began. Obviously the property man's phone call had been from last night's reception: Order had had no trouble setting up a meeting when he'd phoned.

Awkwardly he explained his suspicions about the generation gap, the Wilde's, the Grace's and the missing necklace. Wolf's murder was not mentioned.

At the reference to the missing gemstones Laura reacted impatiently.

"Is that really what this meeting is all about, Mr. Order? A silly piece of gossip which has been in the family for years? I'm surprised a man of your position would waste his time on such tittle-tattle."

"So you know about the story?"

"Of course I know about it!" she hissed, visibly annoyed now and attracting the attention of several surrounding patrons. "Even the embellishments."

"Embellishments?"

"The mysterious third thief, who whisked the necklace away from under the noses of the Keystone Kops and the biscuit tin."

In spite of herself Laura was leaning forward, whispering conspiratorially, keen to tell the family legend and Order waited.

"The story is the third man was my great grandmother, Grace Dempsey, who rode a bicycle past the gate seconds before the police arrived. Tom Wilde, subsequently my great grandfather, popped the necklace into gran's basket and she peddled off down the street."

And even if they had noticed, Order decided, the police were distracted by poor crazy Albert Jones running away from them.

"An' the biscuit tin?"

"Family lore has it the necklace was secreted in a biscuit tin like the one's grocers used to have."

"Surely the police would have thoroughly searched Wilde and Dempsey's homes – including tins?"

"I'd have thought so. Anyway that's the family story, handed down through the generations and I can't tell you anymore, Mr. Order. You're wasting your time chasing this fairy-tale."

"I'm deeply obliged to you for clarifying the matter for me, Ms. Andrew," rising with Laura and hoping he sounded suitably chastened.

"Whatever possessed you to track down this improbable story?" she asked as they exited the café.

"Constituent," he lied contritely.

Far from encouraging him to abandon the investigation, Order now had two firm items to work with. The disappearance of the necklace following the robbery was plausible. Who would expect the involvement of a woman on a bicycle?

The second matter was even more important and conveniently up-to-date. Why did Phil Newman tip off Laura Order was going to contact her, particularly as he hadn't told the man that he not Emmie wished to speak with her?

He didn't have long to wait. Newman invited him to lunch and over a well-done steak and tasty red wine eventually came to the point.

"As you're aware, Mr. Order," the accent intruded slightly, "I'm in a minor association with Harris Andrew."

"Which you lied about originally," Order interrupted.

"For my own good reasons which still apply."

"I've noticed – well it would be impossible not to do so – you have been taking an interest in the family too. A question here, a question there, and now coffee with Laura."

"A matter I needed help to clear up," Order began.

"Mr. Order I'm involved in some delicate negotiations with Harris Andrew and I do not want them prejudiced. Am I being clear?"

"I don't see how my questions over another matter entirely should cause you or your negotiations any concern."

"Well I do and I ask you to stop your prying." Here Newman looked coldly into Order's eyes. "Canberra's still a relatively small place, particularly its diplomatic community. Of course people are careful about what they say as opposed to what they know, but sometimes confidences get out. Your friend Madame A, shall we call her, and a hitherto unsuspecting husband would be embarrassed, you will understand."

"So back off, you're saying."

"From my affairs, yes. Your own affairs, Emmie, isn't it, and our mutual friend, are your concern. Now, coffee?"

"No thanks," said Order.

EIGHT

It made no sense to break off the relationship or to warn his diplomatic friend. It only would cause unnecessary hurt and alarm. Order was confident they would be moving on shortly and as long as he kept clear of Newman's negotiations with Andrew, whatever they were, the affair was safe, although Wendy Wonder's association with her remained a worry.

It had arisen shortly after VW had achieved the deputy speakership when the woman had referred to their 'mutual friend'. Careful questioning had revealed nothing close from Madam A and Order had decided Wendy Wonder simply was trying to big note herself and infer she was part of the diplomatic scene. Nevertheless …

Emmie was another matter and Order was uneasily unsure if Newman's passing reference to her was an implied threat or not.

Not that threats were unusual. His political life was full of them and remained so.

The safer the seat the more danger you faced from within your own Party was a truism which still applied to him.

Wendy Wonder, his feisty, argumentative and bossy deputy speaker, still sought his job and the Bennett's, Bob and Lorraine, both preselection losers to John Order, shared her desire to oust him.

Even though Lorraine Bennett now held the late Speaker Chambers' safe seat the couples' wish for revenge was unabated. His private life didn't help and that which was known: the involvement with dead bodies, did not he suspected prove popular with all colleagues or constituents. His deputy speaker's still unexplained acquaintanceship with his diplomatic friend also posed a threat if VW managed to meet up with Newman and the diplomats somewhere. Whatever he was Phil Newman was no fool and he would have another pressure point against Order.

With an early election predicted, perhaps as soon as later this year, he could not afford unnecessary risks.

"With Lorraine Bennett in parliament the sisterhood is appeased for the moment," his friend Rob Glasson, who as Government Whip kept a careful eye on these matters, said confidently over a rare private lunch in the still threatened parliamentary dining room. "At least as far as we are concerned."

"The marginals?" Order asked, remembering Glasson also was a target but held a safe seat.

"The marginals," Glasson confirmed. "New tactic. If they can win a couple more seats they can trouble us in the Party room."

And all with a straight face and a friendly smile. Given these deadly undercurrents, Order puzzled, how did political parties stay afloat?

"Anybody need help?"

It was not called branch stacking. Exercising a democratic right to participate or some such euphemism, but a sudden influx of ethnics or, in the sisterhood's case, women, were warning signs and a membership drive was vigorously undertaken to compensate.

"Too early. They're looking at a couple of Opposition seats."

Nevertheless he'd need to re-examine his electoral operations and discuss with Todd, his media officer, more publicity.

This wasn't easy. The day-to-day administration of the Parliament was not newsworthy, any more than being a nodding head behind The Chief for an announcement usually targeting someone else's electorate. There was a limit too for appearances in the social pages hiding a glass and anyway, how many votes did that garner?

Liz didn't think they needed to upgrade electoral activity at present. The autumn winds did not encourage outdoor campaigning and Todd explained he needed time to think out something different to give Order what was seen as useful but not currently necessary publicity.

Nevertheless the absence of created publicity did not mean any known figure went unrecognised, particularly if not acknowledged. Politicians sometimes did their reputations harm by behaviour in public which was not picked up or reported by the media but noted and spread upon the community grapevine. Not that all behaviour was poor or worthy of criticism as he found out that evening.

"What were you doing at the National Library recently?" Emmie asked him over dinner.

The smaller size of the National Capital did not always work to advantage, Order realised, as he mumbled a reply.

"You're still pursuing Mr. Rude, aren't you?"

"It's now a lot bigger than Mr. Rude, Emmie," he replied, relieved no longer to be making excuses or hiding behaviour from staff and friends. He felt liberated and the stronger for it. It was nice to share with someone.

Emmie's reaction surprised him. Instead of anticipated criticism as he explained the story of the Plummer necklace she became more and more enthralled and unlike Gabby Williams and probably Liz, had she known, definitely on his side.

"So it does exist," she said excitedly, almost knocking over her wine glass.

"I believe so, Emmie, but I don't know where to go from here."

Order explained the problem he faced obtaining more information with Sass and Laura closing down contact and his inability to speak with Harris Andrew because he had no business to do so.

"An' now it's more difficult because Phil Newman has told me to back off because he has private negotiations with Andrew he doesn't want conflicted."

"Nothing to do with the necklace?"

"Not as far as I know." Order hadn't considered this possibility.

"And are you backing off?" Emmie asked, doubt in her voice.

"Awkward not to. I can't very well go barging into business discussions which don't concern me on what could be a wild goose chase for a missing piece of expensive jewellery."

Order thought he had explained himself well. There was no way he was going to worry Emmie about a threat, even implied, against her, while explaining his diplomatic association was unthinkable.

"John, while I can understand how you can't approach Harris Andrew out of the blue on something you shouldn't even know about, it's equally difficult to accept Phil Newman wants you to stay away from the man if his negotiations don't involve the necklace."

"How does he know I'm involved?"

"He doesn't, but he's still not convinced Mr. Wolf, Mr. Rude, didn't speak to you on the boat."

Ship, corrected Order silently, but he had to agree Emmie's argument was convincing.

"There's a lot at stake. A man's dead an' the necklace must be worth a fortune if it was fifty thousand pounds one hundred or so years ago."

"No wonder Phil Newman wants you out of the way then."

Within days the situation changed worryingly when at the usual passionate assignation a tearful Madame A confirmed what they both had long anticipated: political developments in her own country had seen her husband recalled. They were to leave within the month and she probably would not see him again with all the diplomatic niceties and possible interstate farewells to be undertaken.

Order's initial regret was mingled with relief the threat of exposure to his growing affection for Emmie and damage to his political career now was replaced by another concern: any threat from Newman would be directed solely through Emmie. With Mr. Rude's murder still unsolved and his troubled association with Phil Newman, Order could not discount the fear he was dealing with a dangerous man.

NINE

"**O**verdoing it a bit, aren't they?" Liz observed, looking at the newspaper headlines.

Another Hotel Murder, they read.

"Howso?"

"Sounds like it's happening all the time, like motor vehicle fatalities."

Another middle-aged man had been found dead in a Civic hotel room by a maid coming to clean. The press were quick to draw comparisons with the Wolf-Scott death without saying why.

"Perhaps they know more – " Liz began.

"Then they'd have said so. Our police aren't usually too tight-lipped an' they need the public's cooperation."

Local radio proved Order right with the midday news reporting the victim was an interstate jewellery salesman and had been stabbed to death.

The jewellery connection interested Order although as he told Emmie it could be a coincidence or a copy-cat crime and didn't advance the search for Creighton Wolf's killer.

"It also could mean Mr. Rude had nothing to do with the necklace," Emmie cautioned.

Or some undesirables who were reputably after him, Order thought.

He made no attempt to contact Gabby Williams with his ideas. If he kept going this way, involving himself in police work, he might as well join the Force. Anyway, the authorities were confident of making an arrest soon and already were speaking to some people of interest.

New Lead in Hotel Murder shouted the headlines several days later.

Police now were investigating possible links with a jewellery display at the National Museum of Australia because the man had been an opal collector.

As the National Capital, Canberra was the site of national collections. Its library, art and portrait galleries, museums and archives attracted many visitors and the Australian War Memorial, looking directly across Lake Burley Griffin to the Federal Parliament, was world famous.

These institutions frequently held exhibitions from elsewhere and, in turn, loaned their own displays interstate or internationally.

Australian opals currently featured at the museum.

Talk about a killer was unwelcome to the National Museum, not amused by suggestions the murder might have a connection with its expensive blockbuster, as these exhibitions often were advertised.

The ACT Government also was put out, embarrassed, and The Chief went on local television to reassure residents and visitors alike the city was safe. Hotels were rumoured to be hiring extra security staff, although what they could do to protect guests in the privacy of their rooms was not explained.

Order's personal opinions wavered. He had convinced himself Wolf's death – or at least his presence back in Canberra – had something to do with the Plummer necklace. Now with this killing he was not so sure.

"They could be unrelated," he told Emmie doubtfully, stirring his coffee in the unit's kitchen. One benefit of the gruesome death was Emmie staying overnight with him.

"Particularly the gap between Mr. Rude and the other."

"You're probably right," Order replied, not wishing to alarm her further a lunatic was loose who only attacked at full moon or particular feast days and might not be heard of again for some time.

And he was proven correct. The killing did stop and although Emmie did not return immediately to her own flat, Order was not rid of Creighton Wolf.

For the first time since they moved into the Speaker's offices the Chamber Pot was back in use, alerting Order to an unexpected visitor. Its movement to another part of the room did not do more than forewarn however, because there was no alternative entrance Order could use in the new premises.

The man sitting in his office probably was in his late thirties, tall, clean shaven, tie, and suit and, oddly, wore a prominent signet ring, which he twirled around in his finger as he talked. His name was Paul Bourke.

Mr. Bourke explained to John Order while he regretted the inconvenience of bringing him back from attending the Monday Party meeting, he was unable to tell him where he was from, only why he was here.

Such an impertinence might have caused a reaction elsewhere but the National Capital was obsessively security conscious. Few doors now could be entered without passing through an electronic checkpoint or revealing a pass, usually for comfort hanging from a chain around the neck. Even toilets were camera covered. So if you were told in Canberra someone couldn't tell you about their employment you accepted they were a 'spook' working in covert operations.

"It's about Creighton Wolf," Mr. Bourke justified.

Like Phil Newman he wanted to know if Order had spoken with the man on the cruise and fiddled with the large ring more rapidly when learning he hadn't been seen in public.

"Bit unusual, isn't it? Not even for meals?"

Order explained the seating policy whereby passengers were not confined to one restaurant table or indeed one restaurant these days on cruise liners and could, if they wished, have all meals in their cabin.

"And he disappeared off the boat in unusual circumstances?"

Ship, Order corrected silently, then told Bourke what he thought had happened.

"Certainly nobody saw him again."

"How ingenious." The signet ring was spinning like an aeroplane propeller.

"What's this about, Mr. Bourke?" Order asked, intrigued by the visit. "I've already told the police all I've told you."

"Rechecking procedure, Mr. Speaker," Bourke excused with a smile. "Thank you for your time and again, my apologies for interrupting your schedule."

Escorting Mr. Bourke to the door, Order realised the Creighton Wolf matter was more important than he had imagined.

TEN

"**A** large signet ring, you say?" Gabby asked doubtfully. "Which he fiddled with obsessively? Interesting."

"I didn't think Bourke was one of yours."

"Nobody else's either." Said quickly.

Curious to know how Paul Bourke had tracked him down as a shipmate of Wolf, Order had inquired of Gabby Williams.

And drew a blank.

"How did he get to see you?"

"Told our attendants he was with security."

"Have a badge?"

"Of course." Doesn't everyone? "We don't keep open house here. What's going on?"

"I can't help you further, John," Gabby Williams said quietly into the telephone.

"I understand an' thanks anyway," Order had picked up from the policeman's tone whatever was going on with Bourke was beyond his jurisdiction.

Obviously Williams knew more than he was prepared to confide in him but even his brief comments raised questions. The security Bourke claimed to represent hadn't been checked, however with everyone holding badges and the Assembly hardly the Department of Defence the attendants couldn't be blamed for letting Bourke through.

And he had presented well, always a good start if you wanted access somewhere and no suspicious briefcase, although the signet ring seemed rather a big standout for a 'spook'. Weren't they supposed to be unobtrusive?

Paul Bourke's visit both worried and annoyed him. It worried because he hadn't been told really why he was being questioned except in the simplest terms and he was annoyed for the same reason. Surely he deserved a more comprehensive explanation, the dignity of his office demanded it.

So Order went fishing. He deliberately talked and puzzled publicly about Bourke's strange visit to him. His voyage with the late Creighton Wolf was sufficiently well known among colleagues, staff and friends so no confidences were breached, nevertheless it took a few days before another visitor presented themselves at his office.

This time there was no introduction. A man of average height dressed in overalls and carrying a blinking machine of some sort announced his name was Stan and he was there to check the smoke alarms.

Order was leaving his office to resume the Chair downstairs when Stan sharply called him back.

"My department understands you've been talking around about a recent visit by a Paul Bourke, Mr. Order," Stan began abruptly.

Order was on the point of laughing. The scene was so theatrical: a 'spook' masquerading as a technician.

"Please stop." Stan continued. "There is no such person as Paul Bourke but another very dangerous man."

"What's this about?"

"I'm not at liberty to tell you but it does involve a local death, which is a measure of its seriousness."

"Then the local – "

"No more, Mr. Order. I came here to warn you to stay out of our business, which I have done, and to ask you a question: did Bourke really have a large signet ring? "

"Yes. Which he fiddled with constantly. Why?"

"His trademark and warning, Mr. Order, so take heed, otherwise you will end up like the other fellow."

Stan shouldered his machine and left the room, leaving a shaken Speaker.

ELEVEN

The lunch hour Administration and Procedures Committee passed in a blur. Established to arrange the order of Executive Members, Assembly and private Members business coming before the House it was often the subject of polite but dogged persistence from the Whips seeking priority for their Party's interests.

Rob Glasson cast several worried glances toward Mr. Speaker during the meeting but refrained from commenting as they returned to the Chamber for the afternoon session, imagining some personal matter was occupying his friend.

Chairing the raucous Question Time was no better, although Order had the chance to vent his frustrations upon Members' offending.

How did Bourke find out he had sailed with Wolf? If the man was as murderous as claimed, why was he walking free? Why was he possibly after Wolf and the other dead man anyway?

And he couldn't mention any of these concerns to Emmie, to Liz, to anybody. It was too dangerous if the twirling signet ring was to be believed.

Gabby Williams was the only person he could talk with without fear or panic clouding a sensible conversation, but he knew he couldn't phone him up after the reproof displayed last time.

A breakthrough in the killings provided the opportunity with a brief press announcement a Commonwealth department now was looking into the death as the man might have been an illegal immigrant. Visitors often overstayed their tourist visas to remain in this land of milk and honey.

"Asian?" This could provide a link with Wolf.

"Not what he seems," Gabby replied enigmatically. "He has a record."

"And Wolf?"

"Wolf stays."

Replacing the now disconnected phone Order realised the missing necklace probably didn't feature in the killings, perhaps just an underworld feud. Wolf's involvement was less clear if Gabby still was in charge of the investigation into his murder.

However the conversation still hadn't cleared up Bourke and the threat he presented, but the man with the prominent ring was the least of Order's worries because danger of another and more immediate sort threatened him in the Parliament with the return of Mike Prentice.

Once his best helper in the successful by-election campaign which saw Order win his 176 majority years before, Prentice, ever the lady's man, had defected to Lorraine Bennett and her failed attempt to subsequently challenge Order for preselection.

He now reappeared as Lorraine's political advisor, a position of privacy and late night tactical discussions which provided them with the opportunity to continue their affair, the same affair which known to Order had spoiled her preselection chances.

Rob Glasson had responsibility for vetting staff appointments to ensure unsuitable people and particularly, relatives, were not employed. As Prentice was neither he passed muster, his previous and probably current association with the new MLA allowed to continue because nobody but Order knew of it. This knowledge itself was threatening but of equal concern was the long running enmity between them over the preselection defeat. Prentice also now was an honorary member of the sisterhood.

These were the immediate worries of Order, but nobody was

entirely comfortable with prospects for the forthcoming election.

The Opposition still was recovering from its loss. True, Paddles Porter in the long history of the defeated had stepped down as leader, but Bob Craddock, his successor and previously education minister, was having trouble holding off a rumoured challenge from Hetty Oxley, their ex-transport minister.

The Government should have been eagerly anticipating the next election and had even considered bringing the date forward. This no longer was the case as it was facing its own problems.

"The sisterhood needs constant watching," Rob Glasson confirmed over a coffee in Order's office, "and now our Young Turks in the youth wing are flexing their political muscle."

"An' The Chief?"

"Fiddling while Rome burns. In fact the comparison with Rome is appropriate with our little Empire restless like theirs frequently was."

"No challengers?"

"None. A lot of disappointed Members who expected more of Keane but our only alternative is our Treasurer and Tony King is seen as a duplicate of The Chief."

"Jenny Fellows?"

"There's no support for the Deputy taking over, John. The big step between bridesmaid and bride."

They both knew the situation could change dramatically when preselections were called. The danger was the sisterhood and the youth wing joining forces, replacing sitting members in safe seats with their own supporters. Such success could lead to any result. And again, not for the first time, Order wondered why some people were attracted to politics. It certainly wasn't to benefit the community.

"Any news on the Harris Andrew inquiry?"

"Still stalled, I understand," his old friend replied, "but as I said nothing will come of it, we're all too deeply involved."

"There's a daughter," Order ventured.

"They're estranged, I believe. She's an environmental freak, thinks we should all live in mud huts and daddy's ruining Canberra. She also blames her father for her mother's death."

"Howso?"

"Reckons he ignored her."

"An' she started drinking?"

"Bit more than that. Something about a curse."

"A curse?"

"A necklace that brings its owner's grief."

"Rob, how d'you know all this?"

"Carol, my wife, knows someone who works with the daughter. When her mother died there was speculation about the husband and the daughter claimed – although not directly – he shared re-sponsibility for her death."

"Because of the curse on the necklace."

"Yep. The daughter said it was a fairy story but the mother believed it. Crazy, huh?"

"An' the husband refused to take his wife seriously ..."

"And get rid of it," Glasson concluded.

"But how could he get rid of something which didn't exist? A fairy story, like his daughter said."

"No idea. It's just what I was told."

Order knew Glasson's wife was a sensible woman not given to imaginings, so her story was credible and led weight to the argument the Plummer necklace did exist, perhaps with a bloody history.

TWELVE

Poor Todd, Speaker Order's media officer, had a hard time of it. Gone were the days when as an Opposition backbencher he had shared Jim Terry with several colleagues by pooling their excess financial resources to afford him.

Now as Speaker he had personal staff including a publicity man or woman, allocated upon the reasonable grounds Order would have more difficulty generating the profile he needed to be re-elected.

This opinion ignored the salient fact if he looked after his constituents in the electorate, maintaining a public face there, attending meetings and functions to which he was invited, he wouldn't need the territory-wide exposure of the daily news.

And it was hard to come by, anyway.

There appeared to be a general view in the media a parliamentary Speaker was above the day-to-day representations which kept ordinary local politicians busy: roads, rates and rubbish as the alliteration went. Ministers obtained publicity simply by being what they were. Opening or announcing matters relating to their portfolios, rejecting criticism of departmental blunders, appearing at conferences, announcing good news but never bad and at all times defending the Government and its policies.

Nothing much like this came the way of a Speaker. Order was a regular at diplomatic functions and hosting citizenship ceremonies, filling in for Ministers at local receptions and sometimes territorial events. No newsworthy stories there.

He was expected however – at least by the media - to participate like other MLA's in 'stunts' as he called them. Sitting in cages,
wearing silly hats, riding bicycles in marathons. He refused them all.

"You'll be seen as pompous," warned Liz, while a crestfallen
Todd wondered what he could do to publicise his boss.

Order didn't see it the same way. All the stunts drew no votes
and in his opinion lowered the status of a politician, if that was
possible. Whatever way you looked at it you were not one-of-the-
boys, you lived by different rules, were expected to set an example.
Even the 'issue' day ribbons of various colours of various causes he
reluctantly wore on a lapel.

He thought all such activities phoney and wished the heartfelt
speeches which accompanied most of this publicity could be trans-
lated into practical help.

Nevertheless he still commanded some respect, perhaps even
influence, which often surprised him and no more so than to be
sitting in Harris Andrew's portable office on a big construction site
near the equally big cross-border development of Ginninderry,
north-west of Belconnen. Despite its size the whole area was silent.

"An RDO, Mr. Order. Rostered day off. I use them to catch up on
paperwork." And to his secretary next door: "No calls thanks, Iris."

Order could see Harris Andrew was much more comfortable
in this environment. Open neck shirt, sleeves rolled up showing
fading tattoos of past years on his arms and big hands with beefy
fingers clasped before him on a littered desk.

"Thanks for coming. Your parliament not sitting?"

"No, it's Monday," Order explained.

"Believe you've been talking to Laura, my daughter?" said
Andrew, getting to the point.

"Well, yes," replied a surprised Order.

"We don't talk but there's an e-mail occasionally. Usually angry
– like the last one. Mind telling me your interest in our necklace?"

So Order explained the involvement, adding it really was a

secondary if fascinating issue to the mysterious behaviour and murder of Creighton Wolf.

"Ah, Wolf," Andrew interrupted at one stage, only to add: "A strange man."

"Why would he be killed?" Order asked at the end of his explanation.

"No idea. Why would you link him with the necklace?" Harris Andrew countered.

"Your late wife thought it was cursed," Order said, trying another tack.

"So she did. Poor Grace. But any curse hardly justifies the murder of somebody not of the family like Wolf."

"He knew Phil Newman."

"So?"

"An' Newman told me to back off prying into his dealings with you."

"Phil Newman has dealings with the family, mainly Grace. What's this to do with Wolf's death?"

When Order did not reply, Harris Andrew added: "You still haven't explained Wolf's connection with the necklace? Surely that's not why he was killed?"

"He knew Phil Newman," Order repeated lamely, "who knew you an' your wife, so I thought maybe Wolf had a connection too."

"Not that I'm aware of." Harris Andrew appeared impatient. "And still no connection with the necklace."

"Your daughter seemed to believe there was a possible connection – "

"Not with Wolf," Andrew interrupted.

"But through Newman," Order suggested, adding: "Newman knows your daughter. He helped me contact her." Well, indirectly.

"She's an adult. She can choose her own friends."

Stalemate and with nothing more to say to each other Harris Andrew thanked him for coming and Order was on his way.

Apart from needing the car cleaned after the drive through the dusty empty construction site and meeting Andrew on his own ground, Order hadn't much to show for the visit. And what he had was negative: Harris Andrew had not associated Phil Newman's business dealings with the necklace and, more effectively than Newman's threats, had blocked Order's further inquiries into linking Wolf's death with the family.

As a bachelor earning good money Order had no need to cook for himself. Indeed much of the food would have been wasted with the erratic lifestyle he led, often not knowing what the next day would bring nor, if the House was sitting, even that evening. Regular takeaways were not healthy and were lonely meals.

Which found him with Emmie in the restaurant of the hotel where Wolf died.

"Why are we here?" she whispered in what because of the hour was an almost empty room.

With nothing better to do the young waitress patiently answered Order's questions about the menu choices and the wines, while Emmie looked on in puzzlement at his out-of-character behaviour.

Having won her trust he finished ordering then asked the girl quietly: "Was this the hotel where the murder occurred?"

"We're not supposed to talk about it," the waitress rebuked. "An' we were so busy with all the visitors."

"The visitors?"

"Mardi Gras, of course." She moved off as another couple entered the room.

"What was all that about?" asked Emmie.

"How Wolf's murderer probably got away," Order said with satisfaction.

THIRTEEN

In terms of keeping the population content and hopefully still voting for them, governments revert to the tried and true centuries old Roman success: bread and circuses.

Bread isn't too much of a problem now, even the destitute are fed by charities, and while circuses have been long banned in the National Capital by various animal rights groups, the intent which was to keep the constituency happy has endured.

Every city works at attracting or creating something: motor racing, agricultural shows, and dance festivals, art exhibitions, marching bands, movie stars and singing impersonators …

The competition is fierce. If somewhere can steal a major sporting event from somewhere else every financial attempt is made to do so. If somewhere's success can be duplicated by somewhere else, though not too close and at a different time of year, then so be it.

Which led to Mardi Gras.

Replicated from around the world, the centre of the city, Civic, was cordoned off, decorated with banners and flags and for three days and nights given over to fun and games. Everyone, locals and visitors alike, were encouraged to wear fancy dress, the weirder the better, with spangles, bangles and dangles. Street stalls were set up, pubs stayed open later and music played continuously. It was a great party.

The Government boasted how successful the event was and how much money it brought into Canberra, although it was silent on how much financial capital went into setting up the extravaganza and which neither the Government nor Opposition wanted closely scrutinized.

Order had missed ACT Mardi Gras, as it was advertised: a corny play on the territory's initials to encourage participants to act up. It was held on a special long weekend Friday through Sunday when the Assembly was not sitting and he was busy with the program ahead for the rest of the year.

In his experience most MLA's also avoided most of the activities. They were raucous affairs best left to the long-suffering police if they got out of hand and besides, how could you obtain publicity if you were in flamboyant fancy dress and masks?

He realised he couldn't find out what the hotel guests had worn. He wouldn't be told by the management but who would remember anyway?

"It doesn't matter, Emmie," Order explained over coffee. "The fancy dress rules were the perfect disguise for a murder."

"How did they get into his room?" Emmie asked intelligently. "Wolf wasn't interested in the dress-ups."

"Perhaps he was drunk or drugged outside." He wondered if he dare ask Gabby Williams.

"Perhaps. If not why open the door to someone you couldn't recognise in fancy dress?"

"Unless you were expecting them but not all dressed up?"

"The fancy dress was to get out, not to get in?"

"Exactly. You would stand out and therefore possibly be remembered if not dressed up." He wondered how Wolf died, whether it was slowly or quickly. Stabbing, if the news leak was true, sometimes took time and was messy. Would Gabby tell him?

Which the policeman declined to do when next morning Order explained his theory about dress over the telephone.

"We came to the same conclusion, John," was all he said to the murderer's escape plan.

What Gabby Williams did not also tell Order but the media claimed was a breakthrough in the case was an unidentified person had been asked in for questioning by the police.

An angry Harris Andrew added more specific information in a phone call as Order was going downstairs again to the Chamber.

"Phil Newman's been called in again. His car was picked up by security cameras in the hotel's vicinity the night Wolf died. He had an alibi, dining with my daughter, but he's been asked not to leave Canberra, which is bloody inconvenient for our business dealings."

"Overseas, Mr. Andrew?"

"As it happens, yes. However I wondered if you knew your Minister for Police, y'know mates, and see if you could get him released?"

Order's silent reaction was mixed. So your business dealings can proceed. He's only in for questioning. And the big one: try to influence my old friend, Tim Forbes, to interfere in a police investigation?

"Sorry, Mr. Andrew," he lied. "I don't know the man. As Speaker I'm very removed from the Ministry."

"Worth a try. I'll have to use my own contacts." And rang off.

Order sat through the Assembly deliberations until the lunch adjournment hardly paying attention. Fortunately matters before the House were largely procedural or Opposition responses to legislation, an occasional amendment, both usually uncontentious, and debunking the claim all parliamentary debate was a rehearsal for Armageddon.

Returning to his office, Order found a phone message: *He's out and OK to travel.*

It was on a whim arising from something Harris Andrew had said earlier that Order foregoing lunch drove to the tall apartment building along a Northbourne Avenue still denied winter sunlight this late in the season.

Newman's vehicle was in the visitor's underground carpark, the

PIN numberplate prominent. It could have been enough but he decided to check Phil was visiting Laura and not someone else in the expensive rabbit warren. When the door finally opened Order saw a door ajar deeper inside the unit and part of an unmade bed.

"What d'you want?" demanded Laura. Without her glasses her face was much plainer. She was wearing a dressing gown and her feet were bare.

"Nothing now, "replied Order, turning back to the lifts.

* * *

"I'm a bachelor, a single man, like yourself, Mr. Order. If I form an association with a woman – like you do with your Emmie – surely it is no business of anyone else?"

Order was embarrassed and annoyed by the sensible, unemotional voice on the telephone. Newman was making perfect sense, yet he knew the man was lying. Any association with Laura was not – and Order was surprised to acknowledge – anything like his own association with Emmie.

"Not if it's genuine," he found himself saying.

"Of course, Mr. Order," the smooth logical voice continued. "Thus your unwarranted intrusion into Laura's unit is unforgivable."

"It had nothing to do with your love life," Order protested, forced to defend.

"I hope not," replied Newman. "But our Madame A has less than a month now to leave us without any blemish on her husband's diplomatic reputation."

"What d'you want, Newman?"

"Same as I've always wanted. Stay out of my activities." And the phone went dead.

Order was not yet free of his perhaps ill-timed and certainly ill-considered visit to Laura's unit, because the woman herself phoned her objections. Laura lacked the calm understated approach of her lover.

After her raving about the invasion of her privacy, which puzzled Order as he had not invaded her home, Laura explained the real bonding between them

"Phil and I are committed environmentalists. We recognise the threat to the earth – "

"But he's in property," Order interrupted.

"Only in sustainable building. Solar powered, self-sufficient water, that sort of thing. The construction of which is environmentally friendly and upon which our future depends. He's unique and I love him."

He certainly is, agreed Order, again on a dead phone.

FOURTEEN

"**E**mmie phoned," said Liz, placing the message slip on his desk along with a cup of coffee after he returned from another torrid and barely manageable Question Time, where he had narrowly avoided throwing out two Members.

"Did she say what she wanted?"

Unlike his earlier girlfriends, mistresses, lovers, Liz knew of and liked Emmie. They sometimes chattered before she was passed across to Order on his private landline which bypassed the formidable Beryl.

He regarded the acquaintanceship as another step toward his own closer relationship with Emmie.

"Not really, but she's been phoned by Laura Andrew."

"What was all that about?" Order asked when he contacted her later in the afternoon.

"She wanted me to ask you to get out of her life," Emmie said, coldly he thought. "You're not involved with her too, are you, John?"

The qualification sounded a warning, he thought. On one hand it could refer to Emmie or, worryingly, someone else.

Order vigorously defended himself and was relieved when Emmie accepted his explanations with equanimity.

"Came across as very strong on the environment and how none of you politicians cared."

So how could she be an item in my life, Order wondered, but instead asked how Laura had contacted her.

"Through Phil Newman, I suppose. I gave him my business card." Like anyone starting up these cards were scattered like confetti, Order knew.

"She and Newman are a couple," Emmie explained.

"I know," and Order told of his visit to Laura's unit. "I wouldn't have let you go to the door in your dressing gown," he concluded.

"And I wouldn't have gone at all," she said with a naughty giggle, ending the conversation.

He was turning to his overflowing in-tray when Liz came back, ostensibly to collect his empty coffee cup.

"I've had Beryl in tears earlier, John," she said quietly, addressing him in the informal manner they shared when alone.

"Mike Prentice is making a complaint to you, Mr. Speaker, at her bossy way of dealing with people contacting the office."

We both know it's Lorraine Bennett MLA making an indirect attack upon me through my staff, Order decided, but confined himself to a low grumble he'd never get any work done if there wasn't an efficient person to vet his callers.

He was repeatedly surprised at the expectations of his power and influence ordinary people vested in him. From a personal line to the Governor-General of the Commonwealth of Australia to an ability to arrange cancellation of speeding and parking tickets, people tried to approach him.

Others bypassed the usual channels and made representations on matters concerning Minister's responsibilities: ignoring Eric White to get their out-of-area child into a preferred school or attempting to seek Order's endorsement for a scheme which would save Treasurer Tony King millions of dollars.

Beryl was invaluable in sorting out these hopefuls, firmly but politely directing them to the correct department or Minister's office and occasionally suggesting they seek medical help.

"Beryl has nothing to worry about."

"What do we tell Prentice?"

"To put his complaint in writing."

Which generally settled matters. Many people were averse to putting on paper what they freely expressed out loud. A written complaint also had the advantage it could be carefully analysed and dissected until, in the hands of a competent experienced rebutter, there was no grounds for criticism at all. The public service and through it a government's office staff, was seldom wrong.

"Laura asked me to coffee," Emmie announced over dinner.

"When was this?"

"When we talked."

"And?"

"I accepted today." Emmie took a nervous sip of wine.

"She trying to convert you to mud huts an' vegan food?"

"Vegetarian. She's rather lonely, I think. Newman's not always around, she estranged from her father – "

"Mother's death," contributed Order.

"She blames him, yes, and thinks he should have been more attentive second time around."

"His first wife died while they were in Sydney," Emmie added in reply to Order's puzzled expression.

Emmie believed Laura had a love-hate relationship with her father. She was proud of his success, climbing from nothing, but did not realise the cost this effort could wreak upon family relationships. She also wanted him, which might have contributed to the estrangement, to donate much of his considerable company profits to conservation.

"Perhaps she took after her mother," was the only excuse he could present for such a crazy wish.

"Not too much I hope," Emmie said, the fish and its lemon butter growing cold on her plate. "Her mother had a breakdown after Laura's birth and hadn't recovered."

"So she drinks and worries about a curse on a necklace."

"She was getting worse apparently before she died. Although

Laura blames her father for Mrs. Andrew's death because he paid her no attention, she concedes her mother was very difficult to live with. In fact, although she didn't say so, I think it was a reason for Laura moving out."

"She certainly opened up with you, Emmie."

"As I said I think she's lonely. Maybe she found in me a kindred spirit. Single, independent, semi-professional, youngish woman …" Emmie's voice trailed off and she looked intently at her food.

Don't go there, Order warned himself. At least not now. So he asked why not get rid of the necklace, if it exists and was causing so much trouble?

"Her mother believed it had to stay in the family, it was part of their heritage for better or worse."

"Are you seeing Laura again?" he asked.

"I can make it my business to," Emmie responded. "Have you something in mind?"

"Well if you do, would you – " Order began, topping up the wine glasses.

FIFTEEN

It was the following week before they drove to Sydney – a fortunate coincidence which resulted from another coffee talk with Laura and an Assembly non-sitting week.

Emmie hoped to talk with several companies who might use her fledging business in Canberra, while Order sought people who might have known Harris Andrew. He only allocated a few days however because as required by Assembly rules the Deputy Speaker should be in the ACT and was in charge if the Speaker was out of the Territory.

As there was no way he would leave VW in charge longer than necessary during sittings Order asked Liz to keep in touch through his unpopular mobile. Knowing his dislike for the machine and like an old married couple Emmie offered to look after it for him, so he was thankful Madame A had been warned of his absence.

By careful probing Emmie had found a contact in Sydney, an old close mate of Harris Andrew who was a publican in Pyrmont, where, as already known, the Dempsey's and Wilde's also had lived. Leaving Emmie at their hotel to follow up her own appointments, Order set off for the suburb across Darling Harbour.

The capital of the State of New South Wales and his birthplace, Sydney always had a special attraction for Order. But lately this big, bustling vibrant metropolis sitting on the most beautiful natural harbour in the world had begun to frighten him.

There were too many big changes and he experienced a sad nostalgia when visiting.

Roads twisted, looped and climbed around towering buildings so he needed his wits about him, landmarks had disappeared and those remaining like the huge solid wool stores along Harris Street where he now was driving had been gentrified into loft apartments. He knew there were more rail and road tunnels, including another one under the harbour constructed years before, but this hadn't had much effect upon the traffic which was denser than ever it seemed. Perhaps in a futile effort to control this constant stream of vehicles road routes were changing and each time he visited it took seemingly longer to get anywhere.

Order carefully negotiated the traffic lights at the Miller Street intersection toward the foreshore overlooking Johnstons Bay before turning off. All around were tall apartments but the old pub sat sedately upon the corner.

Australian locals were not known for innovative names. Certainly there were some: *The Hero of Waterloo* over at The Rocks, the *Bat and Ball* near the Sydney Cricket Ground, but most were prosaic like *Commercial, Exchange* or any watering hole near a railway *Station.*

Order found a parking spot near the *Ship Hotel* and entered what for this time of day was a quiet time in the bar.

It was an old-fashioned pub, tiled walls, and a few beer posters. The only concessions to modernity were some poker machines tucked away in a corner of the large room like an embarrassment and a blackboard menu propped up at one end of the bar.

The man who served Order his beer was thickset, bald and carrying too much weight for his health. The man he sought Order guessed.

"Mr. Mike Sullivan?" he asked.

"That's what it says over the door," the man replied unhelpfully.

Order explained he'd been showing people over units locally and had called in for a drink when he recognised the pub from what a man named Harris Andrew had told him on a recent visit to Canberra.

Sullivan's attitude changed as soon as he mentioned the name.

"Harris Andrew! I haven't seen him for years! Believe he's a big shot in Can-Berra?"

Order agreed and explained how well Andrew had done but added it was not without tragedy with the recent death of his wife.

"Ah, that's no good," Sullivan sympathised, his T-shirt straining as he leaned on the bar.

"Grace." Order prompted.

"That's it. Grace Dempsey as was. Harris hasn't had much luck with his wives,"

"I don't follow." Order thought it prudent to display ignorance.

"She's his second."

"Oh, I didn't know."

"Yeah. May, I think. Died in childbirth an' the nipper didn't survive either."

"How dreadful!"

"Yeah. Harris sued the hospital or the doctor for negligence an' won. Then he headed for Can-Berra with Grace."

"Quick work."

"Yeah. A lot of work there at the time so he probably thought he could get into it with the money he'd got, but there also was a story he picked up Grace because she was coming into money, big money. Could've been true, she was no oil painting, an' not to speak ill of the dead, you understand, some people thought she wasn't all there."

"Mentally?"

"Of course mentally." Sullivan was scornful. "How else could she be not all there?"

Realising he'd exhausted meaningful conversation Order promised to give regards to Harris Andrew when next in Can-Berra and drove back to Emmie.

"So your suspicions about the death of Harris' first wife were unfounded," Emmie declared.

"Tragic nonetheless. An' Sullivan added two extra items of interest."

"In spite of what Laura claims was the basis of her mother's breakdown perhaps Grace was always unstable."

"Laura's birth might have made her condition worse," Emmie pointed out.

Order had no answer to such womanly speculation so continued packing in silence.

"What was the second item?" his girlfriend pursued doggedly.

"Grace's inheritance."

"The necklace," Emmie whispered.

"Exactly. Did Harris really know how rich Grace was to become?"

"Before he married her," Emmie concluded.

SIXTEEN

"I didn't bother you," explained Liz when he arrived back the next day. "There's nothing you could do from Sydney."

Liz told him Mike Prentice had declined to put his complaint about Beryl's conduct in writing and instead was preparing a petition for lodgement with the Assembly on the matter.

"He can't do that," Order turned and began looking for his copy of Standing Orders.

"I've already checked, John, and I'm not sure he can't."

Together they examined the rules governing petitions: to be lodged by a member – which will be Lorraine Bennett – signed only by ACT residents or citizens, action is within the power of the Assembly to take whatever action requested, a response on such action required by the Minister concerned within three months …

"It can be an e-petition," Liz pointed out.

"No, they'll want maximum exposure for publicity. Ah, here we are."

In the opinion of the Speaker not within the responsibility of a Minister of the Territory or critical of the character or conduct of a person, they read silently.

"Critical of the character or conduct adequately covers Beryl," they agreed. "She's safe."

"But it still creates problems," said Order.

"It clearly states the Speaker has the make the decision under Standing Orders whether or not the wording is out-of-order.

Nobody else. Not even the Deputy Speaker. An' anyway VW would rule in favour," he continued. "I'm asked to rule about something affecting my own staff."

"The wording of the petition's important."

"An' our opponents will recognise that. They will have checked Standing Orders. Possibly they'll make it a more general criticism of you all."

"Maybe limiting our capacity to do our jobs properly and efficiently."

"Thus weakening my hold on the speakership."

"Surely Members wouldn't want our Deputy Speaker in the Chair?"

"Why not? The sisterhood an' their staff would sign up – the latter if they knew what was good for them – an' the Opposition would welcome the opportunity. They haven't forgiven us for breaking with tradition an' taking both positions an' the chaos with VW running the Assembly would increase their prospects of retaking government or so they'd think."

"When?"

"To be effective an' possibly to mount a challenge against me in the Party room they won't rush this. The presentation of the petition to the Assembly, the resulting publicity, maybe reference to a special perhaps stacked Select Committee and its generated publicity, then the findings. This could go on while they build up support against me."

He repeated this discussion to his old friend the Government Whip, Rob Glasson, that evening in his office over glasses of red wine.

Glasson had heard rumours of the petition, the Assembly usually leaked downpours with something like this, but he couldn't offer more comment than admiration for the plotters.

"A petition concerning and directed inside not outside the Assembly," he marvelled. "It really is smart."

"Thanks," said Order, wondering if he should remove the bottle.

"Credit where it's due, John. And it doesn't even have to be progressed if the Clerks' rule it out-of-order. The proposal itself generates its own publicity even before the event. Smart, as I say."

"What about the Clerks?"

"Still under consideration, I'd expect. Could go either way, although they'd recognise your problem."

The Assembly Clerks, polite and always deferential, were fearless defenders of Standing Orders and would allow a constitutional crisis or fall of a government before ruling with any bias. Their loyalty was to the parliament and its institutions.

"The Ministry?"

"Assuming it becomes a Party room issue, the Ministry will sacrifice you without a thought if it prevents a mutiny."

Glasson poured himself another drink.

"Disunity is death," he added unnecessarily.

"I can't sack Beryl."

"Of course you can't, it would play into their hands. But you've got to do something, John. The only advantage you have at present is time, because as we've agreed they won't want to move too fast."

* * *

He didn't bother Emmie with his Assembly problems and made no attempt to contact Newman or the Andrews. Instead he concentrated upon his duties as Speaker, as if by example he was proving himself and his staff worthy of the position. A vain hope, he knew, because like a sick or injured animal he would be abandoned by his own kind if necessary.

Beryl's behaviour impressed him. She must have known about her assembling critics and their real intentions but she continued as before, firmly dealing with those who sought to waste the Speaker's time, those who arrogantly demanded immediate access or wanted to pass on vital information to the government's benefit.

Surely anyone experiencing her in action would respect her loyalty and dedication?

Nothing had changed in the Chamber, moves might be underfoot but both sides continued shouting at each other as normal and his own interventions as Speaker continued to attract a quiet irritated you-stay-out-of-this glared response. Nevertheless his admonitions were reluctantly obeyed, the offender knowing the opportunity to repeat the offence would soon occur again.

Order had gradually recognised the individual behaviour of Members. Those who came into the Chamber, acknowledged the Chair, quietly took their seat and addressed the papers on their desks. Those who moved around talking to others in low voices, sometimes kneeling beside a desk to converse. The Members who came in and immediately began interjecting if someone was speaking from the other side or the sleepers, as he called them, apart from old Finn who always was dozing off.

No, these were normally well behaved Members who were suddenly stirred by some remark in debate and, in Order's opinion, the most difficult people to deal with, their anger genuine not confected and were difficult to control without a withdrawal of whatever offended them by the Member speaking.

He sat watching this diverse group of representatives, himself ready to quickly intervene if the exchanges became too loud or too heated, for it was unwise to allow the disturbance to continue as it only encouraged others to join in.

While he watched and waited Order thought about the tangled web which was the Plummer necklace, its disappearance and the Dempsey-Wilde-Andrew families tied to it.

Had it really disappeared or did it exist? Was it cursed if it did exist or a silly family fairy tale? People seemed to have different and very strong opinions on the subject.

And did Newman fit into this strange puzzle or was his business dealings with Harris Andrew separate from the necklace?

But the issue of interest to him had nothing to do with the necklace, it was Wolf's death and who did the deed.

His thoughts were interrupted. A sleeper had awakened on the Opposition benches and was loudly demanding a retraction from the always provocative George Graham.

SEVENTEEN

As winter gave way to spring so Laura's demands upon Emmie's time increased. Usually it was after work, occasionally a lunchtime meeting, but none of these get togethers showed any consideration for Emmie's own commitments.

"I've tried being unavailable," she complained to Order as they lay in bed in companionable company, "but she just changes the date or time, often to the next day."

"What d'you talk about?"

"Nothing much, that's what is annoying. I thought I could pump her for information about Newman or the necklace, but she isn't having any."

"Does she admit it exists?"

"The necklace? No. it's still a silly family fairy story she dismissed so strongly the only time I raised the subject I haven't tried since."

"Then maybe it is a myth an' her mother was madder than we think for believing otherwise," Order worried, shifting more comfortably in the bed.

"Yet she convinced Harris Andrew, didn't she?"

"We presume so an' for that she'd need evidence."

"The curse?"

"Probably built up as she thought about her late relatives an' her own condition deteriorated."

"But she'd still need evidence to build a case the curse existed," Emmie reasoned.

"Which means the necklace does exist," Order said gleefully.

"Happy now?"

"Over the moon."

"Then take me there too," she whispered.

Much later that night they hatched the plot which inadvertently created a crisis long-term and solved nothing in the short-term.

Order wanted another chance to meet with and question Laura, who not surprisingly was unenthusiastic in spite of Emmie's guarantee she also would be present. Then Laura proposed a dinner foursome with Phil Newman and Order, hardly believing his luck, accepted.

The preparations stalled any more lunchtime or evening meetings while suitable dates were decided accommodating busy schedules and restaurants were tracked down serving Laura's vegetarian food but also could accommodate the appetites of the others.

Laura, sitting opposite Order, was initially wary, answering his innocuous ice-breaking questions briefly until the smooth reassuring presence and comments of Newman calmed her.

It was a round table so all four could see each other and Emmie later told Order how amusing it was watching the two men taking the measure in front of girlfriends.

Order watched as Newman drank wine and ate steak, following a seafood entre, while Laura confined herself to soup and salad and water. Not quite there yet, he thought, of the man's extreme green credentials.

Newman was good with his words, however, and acquitted himself adequately if shallowly on environmental and conservation issues. Laura backed him, occasionally bestowing a soft besotted look upon her man.

Order tried to probe, testing for some weakness in the man's commitment to the brave new world, but was unsuccessful. Everything which was being done to save or improve the environment was supported. Naturally Newman was particularly strong upon human habitation, building and construction, and challenged Order's own resolve.

"You're the Government. Why doesn't your Party speak out about these rapacious developers, John?"

"Like my father," interjected Laura.

Deciding he would kill or at least severely spank – a thrilling thought – a grinning Emmie when they got home for encouraging this stupid dinner, Order blustered he had no authority.

"But you're the Speaker," claimed Newman. "You're influential." His eyes twinkled.

"Not on policy matters," he protested.

"But you're part of your Party room," persisted Newman innocently.

"Well, yes, but not always," he defended.

"Why not always?"

Order explained the complicated rules which could or did apply to Speaker's being privy to parliamentary tactics planned in the Party room.

"You have no influence if you are there?"

Order knew the man was playing with him. The bastard should have been a lawyer.

"Only as one member of the Party room."

"I hope our efforts to promote the environment won't be wasted on you, John – or you too Emmie," with a smile saying you haven't been forgotten in this conversation, "but obviously we must work harder on the Party as a whole."

Order realised the subject had drifted too far away – and he wondered if this was deliberate – to introduce Laura's family and a cursed necklace, which might or might not involve Phil Newman and the dead Wolf.

Over dessert they reverted to mundane topics and departed upon amicable if cautious terms with no suggestion of another meal.

Emmie avoided her punishment, experiencing a fate more

enjoyable because of Order's increasing attraction to her. Resting afterwards they agreed the dinner had been a waste of time and ill advised.

"She's obviously in love with him," Emmie declared with a woman's intuition, Order decided. He agreed while silently believing Newman was conning Laura. The question was why?

"Perhaps he's in love with her too," he began cautiously, "but for other reasons than we believe are the normal."

"I don't follow," Emmie murmured into his ear.

"We suspect Harris Andrew married Grace Dempsey because of a rumoured fortune awaiting her, why wouldn't Newman do the same with Laura after Grace died?"

"So again there is evidence the necklace exists."

"An' now we have a possible link with Newman and the necklace in his business dealings with Harris Andrew."

This was not the only link successfully made by John Order. Rob Glasson contacted him days after the dinner in his capacity of vetting staff appointments to ensure nepotism or favouritism was not employed.

"Les Preen has contacted me," he said as they sat eating sandwiches in Order's office during a lunch hour break. "He reckons he owes you a favour."

"Me? Preen?" Order was instantly on the alert. Les Preen, plump, volatile, gossip, intriguer, troublemaker. If he owed Order a favour when would he seek one in return? "What for?"

"You know Les, wouldn't say, but he thought you might like to know Mike Prentice has been hanging around Clare in Hal Gould's office. Thought I should know too as the personnel officer for parliamentary staff."

Clare, the willowy blonde bimbo from Fearless Leader's office who had been taken into the Minister for the Environment's employ in the time-honoured tradition of looking after those who lost their jobs through electoral defeat or internal upheaval. It wasn't always possible but Clare was decorative, in fact a knock-out.

And devious Les Preen, who knew Glasson would not interfere unless there was a complaint but knew the Whip would pass on the tip to his old mate the Speaker. Indirectly Order had helped Preen some time back with the man's powerful friend, Marek Conrad.

"Thought it might help get Brian on side over Beryl's petition, I'd reckon," Glasson added, throwing his sandwich bag and missing the waste paper bin.

Although the collection of signatures had not begun everyone now knew about the petition and expected it to be approved by the Clerks. Preen's move might have been premature but it was carefully targeted. Backbencher Brian was enamoured by Clare's beauty and although he could do nothing about a relationship, being married with a young family, this did not assume he would tolerate another married man's attention toward his beloved.

"He's provided you with a lever through Brian to influence others," Glasson added.

He's provided me with a bigger lever than Brian, thought Order, retrieving the misdirected ball of paper from the floor. Mike and I are both predators but I'm more discrete.

The following Friday when the Assembly was not sitting Order called Prentice to his office, first ensuring Lorraine Bennett, his boss, was in a committee meeting.

"As you are aware, Mike, fraternisation among staff is neither encouraged nor discouraged in the Assembly as long as there is agreement between both parties."

"What are you driving at?" The voice was cold but uncertain.

"You an' Clare."

"Nothing's going on, we're just friends."

"I hope that's right." He knows who I'm talking about, Order confirmed. "Rumour has it her boyfriend's a black belt judo. No, this is about Lorraine Bennett."

"Why?" But there was doubt in the question.

"Are you still having it off with her?"

"None of your business." Arrogant now.

"Of course not. But it is Lorraine's. Does she know about Clare?"

"We're just friends, I told you."

"I'll take from that reply Lorraine doesn't know about Clare an' she wouldn't take kindly to being in competition with a very attractive younger woman. Then there's Bob Bennett an' your wife, Carol. Where do they stand an' your well-paid job, come to think of it?"

"What d'you want?" Now defeat in the tone.

"Drop the petition about Beryl an' keep away from my staff."

"What do I tell Lorraine?" Panic in the voice.

"No idea, Mike, but then you always were persuasive with women."

Order stood, the meeting was over.

EIGHTEEN

However he did it what had become known as the 'internal' petition did not proceed and Mike Prentice retained his job, his marriage and presumably, his affair with Lorraine Bennett.

Order's immediate Assembly problem was no longer an issue but the party's branches were restless, never a good sign with an election pending.

In fact it was the forthcoming election which caused the restlessness. While Ministers, and for the interpretation of an unwritten understanding the Speaker, were not challenged for preselection, the same could not be said for other Members.

Every backbencher of every Party keeps a watchful eye upon their seat. While it is argued the safer the seat the greater the threat even Members holding marginals by a few hundred votes, a situation in which Order once found himself, were not exempt. The Party executive or powerful branch members always were on the lookout for talent, which did not necessarily also mean political ability but by name alone would attract votes. Sporting legends were especially favoured and feared.

Sitting MLA's who had worked diligently to retain their seats by only a small number of votes consistently from strong opposition attacks found arguments for being replaced upon the hope the 'household name' would increase the margin. This was attractive especially to the Party's finance controllers who could save money in the electorate's campaign expenditure.

Sometimes the preselection struggle was more personal however, and the sisterhood's aim of more women in the Assembly recently had moved from obtaining candidates for Opposition seats to standing against sitting members of their own Party. A similar plan was being undertaken by their opponents led by Hetty Oxley to boost her leadership hopes.

George Graham, the right-wing maverick, and Alex Higgins, a foulmouthed left-winger except when women were around, were the current targets. Paul Severin, the arch-conservative, was another possible but he outsmarted the sisterhood by spreading the rumour he might retire at the next election.

Order hadn't much time for any of them. However he had a loyalty to sitting colleagues, particularly Alex Higgins who held an adjoining electorate and with whom he shared some constituency duties.

"Not that I can do much," Order explained to Glasson, when offering his help. The Whip was keeping a cautious independent eye on the sisterhood's attempts.

"There's the difficulty," Glasson agreed. "You have to support discretely, otherwise they might turn on you, convention or not. Which is why most of the other MLA's are staying well out of it."

"An' what does Bernie say?"

Bernie, the elderly, chain-smoking, cardigan wearing Party Secretary, was a mentor to many new Members. Guiding their unconfident first steps in public life, protecting their follies and advancing their successes. He stayed out of the political arena.

"He doesn't take sides, as you know, John, but he works tirelessly to stop these internal disputes which risk doing damage to the Party. He was the person who told Severin to float the retirement possibility, I understand, so our girls wouldn't waste time and effort on what could be an open seat."

"Pity about the others."

"Maybe they wouldn't listen." Glasson paused then continued:

"But I believe, discretely of course because he doesn't interfere in preselections, Bernie has come up with a counter."

"Howso?"

"Challenging the sisterhood in some of their own seats. Lorraine's one, VW and Julie Davenport, who all will have to watch their own backs now."

None friends of mine, thought Order, but he worried about a possible civil war and said so.

"I think Bernie would prefer small fires which can be quickly put out than a raging conflagration in a few seats."

"Which the media would pick up."

"And fortunately have not to date. Probably because Bernie's defused the fire so far. Not yet news."

NINETEEN

In spite of Bernie's quiet best efforts to avoid a public stoush over preselections, the issue became an indirect threat thanks to George Graham MLA.

Picking up on the rumour the sisterhood, who shared a reciprocated dislike for him, was targeting his seat for a challenge, Graham decided on the same approach as Bernie but not in the same fashion. A move which risked splitting the Party.

A maverick, racist, chauvinist and opponent of political correctness, he nevertheless retained support in his electorate for his honesty and fearless defence of his beliefs. While these usually were portrayed as unpopular his repeated re-election suggested he had more in common with most constituents than his media critics allowed.

Working on the same principle of carrying the fight into the enemy's territory was good strategy, George Graham announced his intention to move a motion in the Assembly which affected every politician: restricting Canberra's population.

As everyone involved in the legislature knew it was a ploy for publicity: the motion would not be debated before the next election. Nevertheless many people in the constituencies did not know this and many held firm opinions on the subject.

Australia's population, both nationally and locally, had been a matter of intense and unresolved debate for years. Like the emotive issues of abortion, euthanasia and same sex marriage, all resolved long ago, population – or overpopulation as opponents claimed – brought forth strong passions.

Politicians hated the subject and avoided it at all costs.

While the earlier matters were largely of a religious nature, overpopulation covered the gamut of society's concerns and affected everybody.

Business argued higher population provided more jobs as more people needed more housing, schools for their children, transport and health facilities, recreation and sporting venues. The jobs these extra essentials created led to more taxes being paid for the infrastructure necessary for the government to build and maintain these services.

The country could not grow nor prosper without more people. Multiculturalism already had helped transform Australia from a narrow-minded, backward Anglo-Saxon outpost in Asia to a wealthy confident representative of progress on the world stage.

Opponents of a higher population did not challenge the successes of the past, especially the benefits of migration. They simply argued it had gone far enough and should stop.

The progress increased population had created now was only of benefit to a small section of society, principally the rich. More people looking for jobs did not increase jobs but kept wages down as competition for existing jobs grew.

Increased population did not populate the country, extra people largely moved into the conurbations of the large cities, straining the infrastructure and increasing congestion. Multiculturalism was a mixed blessing, with crime rising and public security such an accepted part of life you hardly ventured outside your own door. Racism had increased with the claims of the 'wrong' type of migrant coming into the country with large families and being given generous health and welfare hand-outs.

While some opponents of overpopulation advocated cutting government benefits back to the first two children only and there was unease the country was being swamped by people with alien lifestyles, the overall fear was a declining quality of life.

"George has certainly taken the heat off the preselections," Rob Glasson grumbled as he and Order walked back to their offices after a fiery Party room meeting.

"He's placed everyone on the defensive," Order agreed, wondering what position he should take upon what was an impossible choice.

"Including the Opposition, thankfully," said Glasson. "There's no winners here."

"And it's not our call," Order protested. "We can't close our borders with New South Wales."

"Of course not. Only the Commonwealth Government can control overseas migration – if they've the courage to do so with so many voting migrants here already – but they can't do anything about free unimpeded internal movement between the States. I suppose people are trade within the meaning of the Constitution?"

"Section 92, isn't it?"

"Somewhere there, but George knows this. What are you going to do with your branches?"

"Hope it doesn't arise."

"Not much chance of that, John. The problem's been brewing for years. Lots of people are fed up with what they see as the destruction of our Garden City with more and more people coming in."

"You sound like a Greenie."

"We might all have to be to survive this," said Glasson gloomily.

TWENTY

Predictably, earnest attempts to bury George Graham's Private Member's motion in the Notice Paper, still well short of being debated in the Assembly, understandably failed. What was the point of the motion unless it was for publicity and the media obliged.

Locally editorials canvassed both sides of the population argument and pointed out government's had ignored the issue for years. Business organisations defended more immigrants and social welfare groups, while expressing the need to help the world's poor, attacked the lack of resources being made available, as if this would solve the problem. Statisticians on both sides tried to disprove opponent's claims in often difficult to understand figures and percentages.

Somewhere in the middle were the feared public, the silent majority, who through letters to the editor and vox pop television street interviews complained about increased congestion when travelling, expensive housing and crowds wherever they went.

Inevitably, the national media picked up on the topic, again lecturing all political Parties for failure to address the question long ago, without it should be noted, offering a solution.

Developers and construction industry members signed an open letter published in local and interstate newspapers supporting increased population. This included Harris Andrew's name while his daughter, Laura, phoned John Order and harangued him simultaneously against unrestrained, including high-rise, development, the world's overpopulation and paradoxically what the politicians should do to help them by increasing migration.

Although an environmentalist, Laura did not seem to be a sandal-wearing leftie who still called ugly graffiti street art or favoured going bush to live off the land. Unconventional certainly, but a more sophisticated rebel. Phil Newman played no public part in the matter.

His Party branches were Order's biggest worry and as Rob Glasson had warned the issue could not be avoided.

Like many Canberrans he was dismayed at the headlong rush of progress which from the early years of the century had transformed the Bush Capital into a collection of satellite towns of high-rise apartments and offices linked by wider expressways to feed public transport and in which the private car, once the accepted means of travel for work or play, now was only a source of government revenue for fines and fees.

There was no sign of such progress declining either. Over the next few years existing public space would be used up. The Kowen area was under development, as Order knew, and the future alternatives were either going up, an unlikely purchase of adjoining New South Wales land or cutting into Namadji National Park in the territory's south.

The ordinary branch members, inarticulate as most were on the subject, probably were against the untrammelled development which had been taking place so profitably over many years, the surreptitious gradual infill of sections of land with too few people to protest or even bother to protest ...

Yet Order also knew there were members of his electoral branches who welcomed the development expansion up or out. Businesses which made or provided equipment and the skills, who transported goods to the sites, the retailers who fed and clothed the workforce and the commercial organisations with their legal and accounting expertise. It wasn't all developers and builders, no matter how visible their participation might be.

These two groups had to be satisfied somehow and it was small solace to Order his parliamentary colleagues faced the same dilemma, thanks to the sisterhood's mischievous game and George Graham's reaction.

Unlike other MLA's however, Order confronted another threat he could not accurately identify and which might no longer exist, mollified by her victory elsewhere: the rump of Lorraine Bennett's supporters in his Party constituency. Did they still carry a grudge?

"I'm meeting it head-on," Glasson explained to him over Sunday brunch at his home while his wife, Carol, and Emmie were inspecting the kitchen. Emmie's presence another concession to their growing together, hoped Order.

"Howso?"

"I'm addressing George's motion to restrict our local population and explaining it can't be done. We will have to sort out our size some other way."

"Is that possible?"

"Of course. We'll set up a bipartisan committee of citizens to investigate," Glasson grinned and sipped his wine.

Order had cause to remember his friend's suggestion when he was invited to chair a public meeting the next Friday on the subject.

Established by concerned citizens perhaps with help it was held in what many Canberrans regarded as their town hall. Built in Federal Capital style and opened in 1928, The Albert Hall was an historic landmark beside Lake Burley Griffin near Commonwealth Avenue Bridge.

For many years it was the National Capital's only public entertainment venue for dances, functions, plays, musical evenings and talks. It featured a stage and an auditorium seating about 450 people and was a suitable central point for such a community issue. Order, as Speaker of the ACT Assembly, was seen as an impartial chairman for what could be a heated meeting.

To his relief it turned out to be nothing of the sort. People had forgotten Party Secretary Bernie's aphorism: speeches are to inform not to make decisions.

Order was reluctant to participate nevertheless, but his staff urged him to do so, particularly Todd, his long-starved media officer, who finally saw a chance for publicity.

Rob Glasson also saw a chance to set up his citizen's committee and identified the four speakers on the night as the steering group. Unsurprisingly no MLA from anywhere in the Assembly would get involved so he only needed himself to propose its establishment from the floor, its independence from political influence guaranteed by his selfless removal from committee membership consideration.

The four speakers were not contentious, simply repeating with enthusiasm arguments against more uncontrolled development, the unacceptable size and often design of buildings, the crowding and increased congestion. The questions from the half-full auditorium were predictable, the audience largely middle-aged or older. This was normal at public meetings: the young were either too busy with their families or relied upon parents and grandparents to represent their concerns or simply didn't care.

Order's only real job was to stop questioners themselves from making speeches.

If other MLA's were present he could not identify them and no developers seemed to be there either, although they probably sent observers, standard procedure he had been told.

Once the public meeting was over and reported upon in the media and the steering body under the auspices of the Government got to work setting up a citizen's committee, George Graham's attempt to distract politicians from preselections faded away, the population question destined to remain unresolved.

In the months ahead the committee would report to the Government, perhaps with local publicity, then its findings and recommendations would be pigeonholed by mutual consent of the Assembly Parties.

However given the concern the topic had generated in political circles it was no wonder Order again had no time for murder or necklaces.

TWENTY ONE

The sidelining of George Graham's population distraction saw the Parties resume their preselection manoeuvres.

Although principally made up of good candidates between women and men, with affirmative action for the females and merit for the males being promoted, the occasional wild card entered the lists.

These challengers sometimes were viewed with concern by the major Parties, especially if they were popular local figures, sportsmen and women in particular.

It was not their decision to stand aloof from a Party which worried the political administrators, because despite efforts to recruit them most did not have the membership time required, but rather their independence of the machines and their policies.

Many had only a vague idea what they wanted to achieve in the Assembly. Some had a single platform plank like improving health services, with no altruism involved, or stood against rather than for an issue.

Lacking the resources, particularly financial, to mount the expensive campaign elections these days called for, they relied heavily upon a few dedicated supporters and the occasional media snippet, often restricted to the original announcement of their candidature. Even public exposure like corflutes on dual carriageway separations now were banned, thus denying the occasional glimpse of a candidate's face among the cemetery of white signs.

"So if it's not their exposure which worries our masters," Order said, acknowledging the influence of these backroom and largely unknown powerbrokers. "What is it?"

"According to Bernie if they never received a column inch of publicity, they'd still be a threat," Rob Glasson explained. "Their very names on the ballot encourages voters from the anti-establishment crowd."

"Thus reducing the margin of victory."

"More than that. In a close contest their preferences could be crucial. We'd be better off if none of them stood, then we'd have a straight fight between us and the Opposition."

So much for democracy, thought Order.

It was a depressing subject the tactics employed to obtain power, so he asked his friend if there were more developments in the Kowen inquiry.

"As I understand Andrew's still stalling."

"Still going overseas?"

"No idea, but nobody's game to push him, he's a lot of political clout in Canberra."

"Maybe that's the plan," Order exclaimed. "If this stand-off continues long enough, we'll have an election an' the inquiry will lapse!"

"We'll make a politician of you yet," Glasson laughed. "And not to mention the influence of his political donations."

Like George Graham's population limits, this too was an issue which had never been resolved. Although by law details of payments over a certain amount to political parties had to be declared, there was no compulsory requirement – even if possible – to publicly divulge what these often generous gifts provided the donor.

Order would have liked to approach Harris Andrew to donate to his personal campaign, but he was fearful of upsetting the Party hierarchy in whose financial interests the developer's contributions would lie. He was sure the average voter had no idea of the complicated world a politician lived in behind the public stage.

The contact with Emmie and Laura which had operated before the unsuccessful dinner now had revived and the coffee club regular meetings resumed. Thus Emmie was able to tell Order a delayed overseas trip on behalf of Harris Andrew by Phil Newman was to take place soon. Perhaps Newman at least had decided he had waited long enough.

"Where to?" he asked, mildly curious.

"Hong Kong, I believe."

TWENTY TWO

The telephone call fortunately came after a condolence motion on somebody's death. Fortunately because failure to be present in the Chamber was considered poor form although there were no votes in being there.

Order was sorting through the 'blue' as the daily program was known to establish what sections could be safely left to Deputy Speaker VW without creating turmoil in the House.

Wendy the Wonder Woman was often biased in favour of the Government, which the Opposition had been quick to recognise. They responded by baiting her in ways often childish but effective, like turning their backs upon her when she was in the Chair and they were addressing the House. Something they didn't do to Order, perhaps much to her chagrin.

He was surprised to see Liz, his secretary, for the first time in memory at his Chamber door speaking with urgency to an attendant.

"Telephone about your friend, Mr. Speaker," the woman said carefully. Liz was not allowed on the floor of the House.

Calling a surprised VW forward to take the Chair, Order hurried after his secretary to his office.

"Morgen, Mr. Order," said Newman. "Not interrupting anything, I trust?"

"You are. What d'you want?"

"No, it's what you want, specifically Emmie."

"What d'you mean?" Order sensed the bad news he had worried about after Madame A was no longer a bargaining chip.

"Nothing of consequence if you do as you're told."

"What the hell are you talking about? Where's Emmie?"

"Quite safe in my protection," and before Order could reply Newman continued: "Now shut up and listen carefully."

"Where's Emmie, you – "

"Shut up, I said. Follow my instructions if you want to see her again and obviously, no police."

In Order's frightened silence Newman instructed him to get down to Harris Andrew's penthouse overlooking Lake Burley Griffin.

"Now!" the man commanded and disconnected the call.

"It's Emmie, Liz," he told his worried secretary. "I've got to go. Tell the Deputy Speaker I've an emergency."

He was met at the penthouse front door by Newman.

"Where's Emmie," Order began belligerently.

"Safe. No need to be angry."

Closing the door Newman turned his back upon Order and led him deeper into the residence, up the death staircase and into a study. Here Harris Andrew was waiting, sitting behind a cluttered desk, something Order was not invited to do.

"You know each other." Newman asked politely. "Of course. Then we can begin."

"I want the Plummer necklace," he continued, addressing Andrew.

"What's this to do with me or Emmie?" Order interrupted.

"You're here because you're a stickybeak and I don't want any complications in getting away. Your Emmie is my ransom and will be freed as soon as I'm clear. Now be quiet. I want the necklace, Harris."

"What makes you think I have it?" He sounded tired, the big hands rested awkwardly on the desk as if they would be more comfortable holding a hardhat on a building site. Predictably Harris Andrew wore no tie over his business shirt.

"No more lies, please. Grace told me all about its history. She was paranoid about it."

Andrew sat unmoved but Order's sudden reaction drew Newman's attention.

"How much don't you know, Mr. Detective?" he asked sarcastically.

"To the disappearance after the actual theft, Newman," Order answered truthfully, intrigued to know more. "Rumour had it Grace Andrew's grandmother spirited it away on a bicycle."

"More than a rumour. It was true. Grace Dempsey was fiddling with the bicycle's chain outside the Plummer's gate in full view of the driveway. She was moving already when Tom Wilde handed over the necklace, which she placed in her shopping basket and peddled off."

Harris Andrew was looking bored, as if he'd heard it before.

"I suppose Grace Dempsey as Tom Wilde's girlfriend realised she would be under suspicion when the necklace could not be found," Newman continued, relishing the chance to tell the story, "and she passed it to her father, Bill, for safe-keeping."

"Where Bill hid the necklace nobody knows. It simply disappeared for a couple of years until an unrelated event brought it back to Grace Dempsey."

Her father was a carpenter at the Garden Island dockyard and also moonlighted if he could for extra money, Newman continued. When a foreman at the dockyard offered him extra work building kitchen shelving he accepted and agreed to visit his home at Watsons Bay.

It was afternoon on 3 November 1927 when Bill Dempsey boarded the wooden ferry *Greycliffe* running down harbour to his destination. Off Bradley's Head the 7585 ton Union Steamship Royal Mail liner *Tahiti* en route to San Francisco sliced the ferry in half. Some 40 lives were lost, over 50 injured, including a seriously hurt Bill Dempsey, who had been in the ferry's men's smoking saloon.

Bill knew he was dying and told Grace the whereabouts of the necklace, now stored in an old biscuit tin.

"So it became Grace's problem. With Tom Wilde in prison for the theft she was ill-equipped to deal with the jewellery. She decided to hold onto it until as agreed her boyfriend was released. In her favour was the fuss had died down and probably the insurance had been paid."

"However when Tom did get out, there was a war on. No time to sell necklaces so they decided to wait. Then Tom joined the army and was killed in an accident in New Guinea."

"Leaving Grace pregnant with a boy, Arthur."

"You have been doing your homework, Mr. Order," Newman said appreciatively.

"Grace clearly wasn't competent to sell the necklace, so when she died she passed on the biscuit tin to Arthur, who when he died bequeathed the necklace to his only child, soon to be Grace Andrew."

"No sudden death for Arthur?"

"Not if you discount a heart attack at sixty and a life of boredom as a tallyclerk on the wharves."

"Yet Grace was paranoid, you say?"

"Completely. After her great grandfather and grandfather's untimely deaths she was convinced the Plummer necklace was cursed. She even blamed her mother's memory loss on it."

"You're very well informed."

"I told you, I'd done some work for Mrs. Andrew, property matters, and we became friends. She was a lonely woman," here a scowl toward Harris Andrew, who had not moved during the story. "I think she wanted to share her fear with someone – "

"Childish rubbish," snapped Harris.

"She didn't think so and one day while still reasonably sober, she told me everything."

"Old Plummer was a tight fisted shipowner," Newman continued. "He counted every penny sailing his merchant fleet an' employed the cheapest crews, usually lascars from India. His ships were known as Poverty Plummer's everywhere on the high seas."

"Of course he didn't stint himself or his wife, for that matter, hence the necklace an' perhaps the curse from his scores of poorly paid sailors."

Interesting it was not the owner but the object, thought Order, which carried the threat.

"How did Sir George Plummer die?" he asked.

"Natural causes. But he didn't possess the necklace by then, the Dempsey's or the Wilde's had it."

And the risk was transferred.

"An' Wolf?" Order thought he might as well have the full details, there did not seem to be any danger.

"Ah yes, Creighton Wolf. I had some dealings with him and we thought we could work together selling the necklace. He had contacts in Hong Kong and we decided to use them. The stealing, embezzlement, rumour was a smokescreen I put around for Creighton to leave the country. He had some unsavoury characters who were after him apparently."

"He needed a new identity?"

"Exactly. A visit to Hong Kong conveniently provided him with a contact for the necklace sale and a new passport."

No wonder he gave Order such a searching look on the cruise. Mr. Rude thought *he* had been spotted.

"So he returns as Walter Scott, reports on arrangements in Hong Kong an' gets killed for his trouble."

"Seems so," Newman replied guilessly. "We met, confirmed arrangements, then he was dead."

"What arrangements?"

"I was to obtain the necklace, then Creighton and I would take it to Hong Kong."

Because you didn't trust each other, Order thought.

"Now," Newman continued, "I have to do it all myself and

couldn't too soon after the murder, it would've looked suspicious."

"Howso?"

"Because Wolf was involved in the negotiations with Harris."

"Why go to all this trouble? Why haven't you sold it here, Mr. Andrew?"

"For the same reason Harris hasn't sold it," interrupted Newman. "It's stolen property. Statute of limitations or not, the media would enjoy this hundred year old mystery now featuring a prominent local businessman."

And who is before an Assembly committee for possible fraud, Order reminded himself, noticing for the first time discomfort on Andrew's face.

"It's still theft," said Order, nodding to Harris Andrew.

"Under the circumstances I've just outlined only if he still wants the necklace. And you're here because I needed to keep you quiet until I've moved on."

"Emmie – " Order began threateningly again.

"Is quite safe and no harm will come to her if I can leave safely. My word." He held up three fingers, Scout-wise.

"You want the necklace," confirmed Harris Andrew.

"Please."

"He makes a convincing case, Mr. Order." Andrew said wearily. "Although I reject the curse idea as superstitious rubbish the Plummer hasn't brought my late wife's family much joy over the years. I have more than enough money now and have no use for it."

As he spoke he rose and moved to the back of the study where a reproduction of Constable's *Hay Wain* hung on the wall. Whatever he did the painting swung open to reveal a large obscured safe. Some quick fiddling and the operation was concluded.

Harris Andrew held a biscuit tin, speckled with age, in his hands. Silently he came back to the desk and wordlessly handed it across to Newman.

Unable to resist Newman tugged at the square lid which opened to reveal yellowing newspaper. Pushing it aside he let out a happy sigh. Order could not see the necklace nestling deep in the old paper, but if greed has a facial expression Newman demonstrated it. "Thank you," he said.

"Emmie," Order began.

"Not yet, Mr. Order. I'm not letting you have her until I'm clear of here and the police – not that I've broken any law, mind you. As you witnessed the handover was voluntary."

And as if he expected to be stopped Newman backed to the study door and carefully opened it, putting a hand behind him to do so.

"Don't do anything stupid," he cautioned. "After I'm clear I'll contact you through your office, Mr. Order, and tell you where she is."

The door closed and Order looked across the desk at Harris Andrew.

"Police?" he suggested.

"No!" Andrew said emphatically. "I don't want them and we've your lady to think of."

"So we wait?"

"We wait. My guess is he'll head for the airport and Hong Kong."

"I can't wait eight or nine hours," Order exclaimed.

"You probably won't have to. Only a couple of hours, I reckon. Once he's out of Australian jurisdiction, in the air, he'll contact you."

"You're very relaxed about this, Mr. Andrew."

"I've really nothing to lose, Mr. Order. Before Grace died I was going overseas for medical treatment, which might or might not save my life. Otherwise I'm dying."

"Otherwise?" Order caught the resignation in the tone.

"I'm not sure I'll bother now. Grace dead, my daughter Laura estranged." A wan smile. "Perhaps there is something in the Plummer necklace curse."

Andrew heaved himself from behind the desk. "It's Thursday. Fatima's day off, Mr. Order, but I think I can find some coffee."

TWENTY THREE

True to his word and Harris Andrew's prediction, Newman from a Hong Kong flight contacted Order's office where he had spent a frustrating and nervous several hours with worried staff.

At the suggestion of Liz, concerned about the carpet wearing out, Order unusually was in the Chair half-listening to an Adjournment debate, when the call came through.

Accompanied by Gabby Williams and Sergeants Shanks and Varna, Order perhaps unsurprisingly was directed to Creighton Wolf's old office.

Williams' swapped cars at the Assembly, both to allow Order to direct the posse and, as he suspected, to brief him on confidential matters.

"The hunt for Paul Bourke has been called off," Gabby began.

"Howso?"

"He's overseas now. Interpol's job, tho' they've never caught him yet, I'm told."

The policeman explained the Feds, as they were generally known, had been obliged however grudgingly to provide some reasons for terminating a search which involved the local force, irrespective of who was running the show.

Wolf, probably because of his money laundering activities although the reason was unstated, got himself involved with some very dangerous people, including Mr. Signet. He wanted out but realised the only way to escape, correctly as matters developed, was to disappear.

"So he faked it," Order said, manoeuvring across traffic lanes on Adelaide Avenue toward the Kent Street overpass. And with the sale of the necklace he had the money to start again, he thought.

To make himself even safer, Gabby continued, Wolf foolishly wrote a letter to the federal authorities before he took off for Hong Kong. In it he named the people he was dealing with in whatever was going on.

"Their man was the person murdered here," Gabby said solemnly.

No wonder Wolf wanted to disappear faced with such ruthlessness, a shocked Order decided. Mr. Signet had been sent to kill off anyone who could or might talk. What were they up to, he wondered aloud, waiting his turn at the overpass traffic lights.

"I wasn't told, John, and you were lucky you had no contact with Creighton Wolf on the boat."

Ship, he thought, but how did Paul Bourke know I was on board?

"The same way he knew about Wolf's letter naming names. These are powerful people, John, with all sorts of contacts. Are we there now?" as Order turned into the Deakin business area.

"Upstairs," said Order, leaving his car blocking the narrow circular road and sprinting toward the building's entrance and up the stairs.

Shanks kicked in the office door glass and in the gathering gloom of early evening Emmie was found, bewildered but comfortable with a flask of coffee. The phone had been long disconnected and her mobile confiscated but the lights still operated, allowing for a tender reunion while the police stood around in embarrassed silence.

Order found himself holding Emmie with the same fierce determination with which she was holding him. Hitherto this behaviour had been associated with passion but this was different. He had genuinely missed her, was worried for her. It was much more than sex.

A brief discussion proved how well Newman had played Emmie and Order. Telling the other was in danger unless they did what he directed. Newman didn't need to exercise force, but his psychology betrayed more about themselves than they each realised.

"So they've gone," Williams observed.

"They had their packed bags waiting," Emmie explained.

"Nothing more we can do here," said Williams. "Let's get your friend home."

TWENTY FOUR

"So what happened?" Order asked driving Emmie to his unit. "How did you end up being" he baulked at kidnapped "with Laura."

"She asked me to help clear out an office, collected me from work. I didn't know it was Mr. Rude's until we got there."

"And then she told me you would be in danger if I left before Newman arrived and we would have to wait," Emmie continued.

"And?"

"And nothing. She said they were flying to Hong Kong to sell the Plummer necklace. The packed bags were there when we arrived. It was so well organised I was intimidated."

German efficiency, Order decided.

"So Laura admitted the necklace existed?"

"Yes, the fairy story claim was to put you off, but it didn't work."

"No," he began.

"So I've decided to take up an earlier offer you made and move in with you."

"It's messy," he agreed, "keeping clothes in two places."

"And somebody has to keep you from chasing dead bodies, you could get me killed."

"Is that a proposal?"

"If you want to read it as such."

"Then yes," said Order, slowing down the car's speed in case her reaction caused an accident.

Gabby Williams wasn't as accommodating the next day, drinking tea in Order's office.

He rebuked him for not calling in the police until Newman made contact from the aircraft however it was more of a formality, Order thought, with Williams realising the threat to Emmie had been unresolved at the time. For the same lack of evidence of a crime the aircraft had not been diverted in Australian airspace.

"We will try to keep you both out of the story," the policeman promised. "The media should have more than enough to talk about, I'd think."

Gabby Williams paused.

"I saw Harris Andrew earlier about his daughter " he continued, "and he confirmed there was no compulsion in handing over the necklace to Newman, so no crime has been committed."

"What about Creighton Wolf's murder?"

"No direct evidence pointing his way. A motive of sorts. The Plummer necklace would be worth five to five an' a half million dollars – maybe more - in today's values. Enough to share, you'd think, even at a reduced rate, but then Newman claimed Wolf had people after him, which was why he wanted a new identity and money."

"So he got away scot free to Hong Kong."

"For what it's worth, John. We found the biscuit tin in his car at the airport, by the way."

"For what it's worth, Gabby? I'd say it was still worth a fortune, even at the usurious rates of a Chinese fence."

"John, Harris Andrew told me more this morning. The Plummer necklace was paste. It's worth nothing. After buying it but before the theft Plummer got into financial difficulties, short-changed on shipping war reparations perhaps, and had to sell the necklace. But nobody was told. These people were doyens of Sydney society. It would have been personally humiliating and perhaps bad for business. So Plummer sold overseas and had a replica made."

Order could not be sure what amazed him more: the story itself or listening to the longest explanation he had ever heard Williams make.

"So how long – "

"Before the replacement was identified? Grace Andrew's father."

Poor dismissed Arthur, waterfront tallyclerk. The first of the family to have the opportunity to sell the Plummer finds it's worthless so it becomes a keepsake.

"Surely Grace Andrew would have known?"

"Probably, but she was focused on the curse of the necklace."

And Harris Andrew couldn't get rid of it while his wife was alive because it was a family heirloom, cursed or not, the poor woman imagined should not be destroyed. Perhaps she even feared for someone else's safety if they owned it.

"An' Laura?"

"Laura didn't want it personally. She only wanted to sell it off for her green activities, which would have caused a scandal: the theft, the fake and the reputations. So she was told nothing, but believing the necklace was genuine tried to put you off for her own reasons, so Harris Andrew reckons."

Then on Grace's death the opportunity presented itself to pass it on and Harris took it.

"So what happens now?" asked Order snapping back to reality.

"Nothing. Case closed. Meantime I've still a murder to investigate," and Williams rose from his seat. "Thanks again for the tea."

The policeman was lumbering toward the office door when Order called to his retreating back.

"Gabby, what day did Grace Andrew die?"

"Thursday."

Fatima's day off.

"Gabby, I think Harris murdered his wife."

Hardly pausing Williams briefly turned back: "And we'll never prove it, John."

TWENTY FIVE

"Little realising Laura was a party to stealing it," Order marvelled later, explaining the conversation to Emmie.

"Leaving the two environmental love-birds sitting broke in Hong Kong," Emmie said with ill-concealed pleasure.

"It's not inexpensive – as we know," Order quickly added, remembering Emmie's spending spree in the fabled destination but not wanting to embarrass her.

"Not if you want to enjoy yourself," was the response.

So what would they do, Order wondered? He doubted they would hold return air tickets to Australia and imagined Newman at least would have liquidated most of his assets here. The current value of the real necklace would take him anywhere in the world.

And with or without Laura.

Although the woman clearly was in love with Newman he was sure the man was using her and would dispense with her services ASAP.

This now was more easily said than done, because although Order had no doubt he was ruthless enough to abandon her to the Australian Consulate-General in Hong Kong and, ultimately, the financial help of her estranged father, he needed her more than ever.

"Laura's probably his ticket out or back here," Order decided. "He has no money or very little so he can't send her home alone or take off by himself an' they're supposed to be a couple."

"Like us," Emmie said sweetly.

After the recent adventure and true to her word Emmie had moved in with Order. However like so many lovers who decide to cohabit, basic domestic living called for adjustments over seven days and nights a week unforeseen by either of them: toothpaste, mouthwash, pantihose and socks in the bathroom all contributed.

"Perhaps it's not as bad as we think for them," said Order, not wishing to revisit more prosaic issues like continuing to send his shirts to the laundry instead of ironing them himself and something Emmie adamantly refused to do.

"After all, who knows about the Plummer necklace, fake or not?"

Which explained why Laura and Newman were back within a fortnight, to all intents and purposes returning from an Asian holiday like other Australian couples. Order and Emmie would not have known of their return if Laura had not tried to revive the coffee club.

"After what happened to me, I thought it rather brazen," Emmie complained.

"But nothing really did happen, did it? That's what's so frustrating. Nobody's guilty of any crime."

"Two deaths however. Mr. Rude and Grace Andrew."

At Order's suggestion Emmie recontacted Laura and they met for coffee.

"Waste of time," she reported. "No Newman, no necklace, no saving the world or thank you daddy for saving us."

"No Hong Kong?"

"An embarrassment, she admitted, and I wish I could have seen it. She added a bit then changed the subject. I got nowhere."

Leading Order to try another tack.

TWENTY SIX

"**E**ven though we're estranged she's still my daughter, Mr. Order," Harris Andrew said in expiation of why he brought them home from Hong Kong.

They were in his study penthouse set at the back of the building, so the magnificent view including Canberra's evening twinkling lights and Lake Burley Griffin itself would not distract from business.

"An' Phil Newman?"

"Haven't seen him since they got back. Perhaps he's uncomfortable being in my debt after what he did, but he needn't be. He helped me get rid of a bloody irritant."

"The necklace."

"The necklace. After Grace died I thought I was free of it but Laura wanted to save the planet by selling it. Newman provided a method of disposal which would avoid embarrassment, even scandal, to the family so I'm grateful to him, not the other way around."

Harris Andrew paused while Fatima, the Filipino maid, delivered two coffees, inadvertently giving Order the opportunity to raise another subject.

"I'm surprised your girl is still with you," he began as the door closed behind her. "She must have been traumatised to find your wife's body."

"She was, when she came home from her day off, "Andrew replied unhesitatingly. "I was still out on one of the sites an' Grace was home alone. Drinking, of course," he added matter-of-factly.

"She slipped?"

"That was the finding. Anyway, what can I do for you, Mr. Order?" The earlier subject was closed.

"Creighton Wolf an' the necklace."

Harris Andrew smiled sheepishly, his big hands fiddling with his coffee cup.

"I wasn't honest with you, Mr. Order, when we last talked about Creighton."

Order waited.

"Wolf was in the necklace negotiations with Phil Newman, but we were only in the early stages when Grace had her fall. That seemed a blessing. All we had to do was get Laura onside and I was rid of it."

"Enter Phil Newman."

"Perhaps, Mr. Order. I don't really know. Their relationship seemed convincing enough to me from the little I saw and was told, but then I'm only an old developer. What I do know, however, is it took time to establish and then Creighton was killed."

"Murdered."

"Whatever. This threw the plans out. At the best we had to postpone moving the necklace in case Wolf's involvement became known."

"But you knew it was a fake."

"I was the only person alive who did so and I thought I had to be careful. Was Wolf's death connected to the Plummer? Keeping him out of the picture seemed the safest path, then you started showing an interest."

"So the confrontation in this office with Newman was a farce?" Order almost added: for my benefit.

"Far from it. Thanks to Grace, Newman knew all about the background to the necklace but she muddled it up with the stupid curse. To make the plan to be rid of it work I had to play a part of being reluctant, but accepting because of your hidden girlfriend, to hand it over."

"Once they had the Plummer and found it was a fake," Andrew continued, "they couldn't do anything about it and I was clear of it too. And nobody had broken the law."

"Except Wolf's death."

"Apparently he was mixed up with some shady characters, but we couldn't be sure he wasn't killed because of the Plummer."

Which was the same motive Order held for Grace Andrew's accident.

* * *

Breakthrough in Murder Case read the headline, continuing on a person had presented themselves to Civic Police Station and made certain admissions.

"It's Laura," Emmie said, handing the washed breakfast dishes – another issue of domestic contention – to Order to be dried before they went to work.

"She told me she was going to do it," she explained. "Give herself up, I mean."

The resurrection of the coffee club had paid off. Laura told her using the fancy dress of the ACT Mardi Gras held earlier in the year in face mask and colourful outfit she had visited Creighton Wolf at his hotel to discuss the sale of the Plummer necklace. But she came armed, negotiations to date had not been successful.

Wolf wasn't as smart as Phil Newman, Order decided, stupidly demanding in advance a share of the proceeds. Newman, he was sure, had no intention of using the money for Laura's environmental crusade but he wasn't about to tell her until the deal was done.

Outraged at his selfishness over the common good, Laura stabbed Wolf to death, re-joining Newman afterwards in a nearby restaurant full of other masked Mardi Gras dress-ups.

"No wonder the police couldn't pin anything on Newman or anyone else over that crazy weekend," Order agreed. "But why did she confess?"

"She explained she justified the killing for the cause, but when the Plummer turned out to be a fake she felt guilty she had taken a life for no reason."

And Order wondered if Laura's mental state was closer to her mother's than realised.

Fortunately there was no need for John Order and Emmie to be involved and Gabby Williams promised to keep them out of the story, which was easier than anticipated.

A prominent developer's daughter charged with murder was news enough without a century-old stolen necklace subsequently found to be paste as the motive and causing embarrassment all round for the fatal deception.

Perhaps it ran in the family but like her paternal great grandfather Laura said nothing about the Plummer when charged and did not provide a reason for killing Creighton Wolf, leaving many people to think sexual misbehaviour was involved. The plain features, glasses and earnest commitment to the environment and conservation convinced them Laura was a prudish virgin protecting her honour.

By surrendering her passport, accepting a curfew and agreeing to live with her father, Laura was released upon substantial bail into his custody – a contentious decision which encouraged mutterings of the influence of big developers like Harris Andrew upon the law.

She's no threat to society, Order claimed, but privately, because he had been kept out of the story. The same could not be said of Emmie.

"She's started the coffee club again," she complained, "and she's seeing Phil Newman."

There was nothing in the bail conditions which prevented their associating and Order knew from his earlier conversation with Harris Andrew he would raise no objections. Nevertheless Order suspected Phil Newman had no choice but to stay close. He needed to protect himself from getting involved in the crime – hitherto he was not an accessory – and if he'd liquidated his business in anticipation of the Plummer fortune he still might need Laura as a meal ticket.

With Emmie as the conduit Order was kept up-to-date with developments, thus he learned while Harris Andrew's health had not improved, he no longer was travelling overseas. Of the Assembly committee's inquiry into the Kowen development there was nothing.

TWENTY SEVEN

If Harris Andrew had been let off the hook the same could not be said for Speaker Order: the sisterhood and their female supporters in the Opposition renewed their call for the closure of the Parliamentary dining room and succeeded in setting up a committee to investigate its operations.

Over the years as the number of female MLA's increased the role of the dining room and its bar had decreased in importance. Although drink driving laws were most often used as the principal excuse the reality was it wasn't an exclusive men's club anymore. There even was talk of turning it into a crèche to compliment the breakthrough agreement in the past permitting breast feeding in the Chamber.

The female MLA's made no secret of their intention to close down the facility, stacking the five member select committee with three women and two sympathetic males, one a teetotaller.

Order himself had mixed feelings. He recognised the convenience the dining room provided, particularly for lunches and for entertaining visiting delegations from other parliaments.

However lunching outside the Assembly did enable Members to be seen in public by their constituents and hotels could provide private rooms to entertain interstate or overseas guests. The absence of the dining room also might reduce the number of irritating evening sittings of the House, which seemed to always lead to fractious behaviour from tired MLA's.

The main danger of a victory for the sisterhood, as Rob Glasson pointed out, was it could encourage them to further changes, although he couldn't think of any new agenda.

As Speaker Order's responsibilities included the dining room and he was obliged to appear before the committee.

The exchange was very polite: you didn't want to get your referee offside. Nevertheless he found the experience heavy going, even with the support of the Clerk of the Assembly and various finance officers.

Try as they might there was no way the losses of the dining room could be hidden or excused. Most damning was how few Members used it. All the female MLA's either had lunch in their offices or coffee and cake, it appeared, with friends outside. Many of the males too stayed away, perhaps in deference to their waistlines. Whatever, it was ruinous to the business which could not be sustained.

Only in exceptional circumstances was a committee inquiry held in private so the media had access to the public appearances if not the deliberations and predictably found good copy. Order liked the old place and reluctantly awaited publication of the report and its endorsement by the Assembly to close it down.

Rob Glasson's fears of encouraging further changes appeared to be confirmed when moves were made to limit air travel to economy over any interstate distance, hitherto restricted to only Sydney and Melbourne, and Members electric vehicles to small cars. The latter restriction was seen as a counter attack because the female MLA's predominantly enjoyed using the larger people movers to transport their families.

"We'll all be on bicycles soon," someone observed ruefully.

Order found the whole tit-for-tat wearying and petty. He missed the electoral forays addressing constituents concerns, which his high position now found him increasingly limited to do. Only occasionally did he have a street sign replaced, mindless graffiti removed or a dangerous build-up of debris in a culvert cleared.

Small matters perhaps, but issues ratepayers were concerned about and formed the real basis of his election – and re-elections. The only satisfaction was that coming from the Speaker these small representations were speedily fulfilled.

A similar problem occurred with speaking engagements, a duty he enjoyed, at Party branches and with local groups. He now was seen as too important for such activities and banished to VIP events where he was hurried into functions to sit with other dignitaries and at any interval in the proceedings just standing around in the green-room drinking with the same people.

Past days of sore feet and worn shoes from pamphlet letter boxing or doorknocking were gone and while he didn't miss them, the opportunity to meet the electorate had been replaced by a be-wildering collection of electronic gadgetry he did not understand but which Liz, Beryl and Todd handled with ease. This kept him before his voters by regular government updates and local newsletters, even if John Order himself rarely featured.

With the anticipated closure of the Assembly dining room another problem was presented to Mr. Speaker: the staff currently employed in the establishment.

Order had noticed before politicians were seldom outspoken where employment decisions were concerned. Certainly on the broader issue of jobs both side of Parliament stood up for the workers, but if a company or organisation collapsed, even one employing thousands, the political response usually was a combined sympathetic shrug and silence.

"So what can we do with them?" Order asked the Clerk of the Assembly at one of their regular meetings, knowing positions for cooks, waitresses and a barman was not part of the usual muster of the Parliament.

"Nothing, Mr. Speaker," the man said brutally, "but we must move carefully, one of the staff is a union delegate and quite militant."

"No openings in the catering or the hospitality industries?"

"They look after themselves and although there is a healthy turnover of staff, particularly restaurants stealing each other's chefs, I can't see them making a special allowance for our people."

"So what do we do?"

"Perhaps we should await the findings of the committee, Mr. Speaker."

Order could not see the sisterhood representatives on the committee being understanding toward the female workers in the dining room, but agreed it was prudent to await the recommendations rather than anticipate an outcome. The last thing he wanted was a demonstration outside the Assembly with banners and speakers denouncing the Government over loud-hailers. And it would be the Government, the Opposition simply would be uninvolved.

So preoccupied with this industrial issue, he paid little attention to Emmie's coffee club meetings with Laura. These, because of her curfew, took place during the day or, for the working-girl convenience of Emmie, at night in the West Basin penthouse castle of Laura's father.

TWENTY EIGHT

"It's a funny set-up," Emmie explained over dinner one night. They still maintained their restaurant evening meals and weekend lunches. Neither had the ability nor interest for cooking the variety of food they both enjoyed.

"Laura and Harris still don't communicate. She's back in the bedroom she had before she moved up to Lyneham and Fatima serves their meals to them separately. Mr. Andrew is in his study most nights and during the day he's out on his building sites, so there's not much chance of them seeing each other. Lonely for Laura though."

"She's not working then?" Order asked and immediately regretted it from the pitying look Emmie gave him, so he quickly asked over her 'hardly' was there any news of Phil Newman.

"Yes, he visits regularly, I believe. Laura doesn't say much but they're still an item."

"Doesn't stay over?"

"No, unlike Mr. Andrew's girlfriend."

"Girlfriend?" Order was suddenly alert.

"Not often, apparently. Weekends, I think."

"How d'you know?"

"Even with two people not speaking but living under the same roof, big as the place is, it's difficult to maintain privacy. Extra dinners, lounge room use, coming home late … "

"Who is she?"

"Laura has no idea. She only saw her once when she was on the balcony above the stairs and they came home. Plump, about Mr. Andrew's height and age, blonde or perhaps white hair. Laura ducked back into her room before they saw her."

No doubt Harris Andrew was lonely and had been for a while. Order recalled someone telling him the man no longer took his wife to functions because of her drinking. Enough time had passed since her death to decently take up with another companion and Canberra always had a liberal reputation for such behaviour anyway.

Nevertheless if Grace Andrew's fall had not been the accident as claimed now a motive existed.

"I wouldn't read too much into it, John," Emmie said, stirring her coffee. "I noticed your reaction when I mentioned a girlfriend, but the case is closed. Mrs. Andrew died in an accident."

In an otherwise empty unit, thought Order.

"Suppose she didn't, Emmie. Suppose she was pushed?"

"By whom?"

"There's not many suspects. It can't be your Mr. Rude, he was only back here a few days before being killed an' Grace Andrew died after that. There's Phil Newman, of course, with opportunity and motive."

"But who wasn't in the house at the time."

"So Gabby assured me, but I wonder how he knew?"

"Fatima?"

"It was her day off. She wasn't there. Or d'you mean as a suspect?"

"Fed up looking after a drunk, perhaps?"

"Bit drastic but a possibility. Then there's Harris himself or his girlfriend. We don't know if she knew Grace."

"And Laura."

"All have motives, with Newman with the most to lose or so he would think at the time."

"Still does," suggested Emmie. "Although she's on a murder charge Laura's still his best insurance against poverty and old Harris Andrew bears him no ill-will."

TWENTY NINE

"**S**een the paper yet?" Order asked Liz as he passed through to his office.

"Just now." No matter what time he arrived at the Assembly, Liz was there before him. "But I heard about it on the radio news."

It took most of the morning before details emerged and although they were incomplete the information was substantially accurate: the local Electoral Commission had made a redistribution of constituencies.

This was not unusual. By law each electorate in the cities had to be comparable in size, give or take a small percentage. The country seats were different, allowance being made for sparse populations.

The variation in voters causing a redistribution could range from a small decrease, the effect of retirees moving elsewhere, to a considerable increase due to say, a nursing home development or new high-rise units in a shopping centre. As the National Capital, Canberra continued to grow with new housing sub-divisions voraciously eating up green field sites and rural properties despite local protests.

As George Graham's population attempt showed, there was no change in policies, the rates revenue was too important to be dismissed for abundant parkland.

Individuals and political Parties had the opportunity to appeal the Electoral Commission's decisions but the organisation was too experienced to make major mistakes and minor adjustments hardly mattered to what was a numbers game.

Nevertheless every Member protected their existing turf, even if it was a single street, with the vigour of an animal or a bird.

Although the newspaper's depiction of the new proposed boundaries were not clearly defined it was obvious Order's electorate had moved significantly to the west into territory held by his colleague Alex Higgins, who in turn had moved marginally north into the seat of Julie Davenport.

Leaving Beryl to handle the telephones, Order was joined by Liz and Todd over the spreadsheet of the blown-up map.

"That's inconvenient," Todd pointed out.

The large shopping complex of Threeways, with access once shared with his two colleagues, now sat solely in his own electorate.

"Everyone around will still shop there," Liz said with conviction.

"An' Alex an' Julie will have to continue to man the entrances from their own electorates to pick up their voters." With my pamphlets too, he thought uneasily. Was Davenport to be trusted to hand out how-to-votes for Order to his new and probably confused constituents?

"Messy though," Liz agreed, having picked up her boss's concern. "Maybe we should do it for them rather than the other way around?"

"I'll need more workers." Would Julie Davenport necessarily trust him anyway?

The discussion moved on from the Threeways manning problem. Liz would have to liaise with Higgins' office and obtain the percentage of votes for the Party at any of his polling booths now in Order's electorate.

Meanwhile Todd needed to draw up a pamphlet introducing the new candidate to Higgins' ex-constituents, arrange a meet-the-Member evening and perhaps a doorknock in the new section. Although he had established there was no Party branch in his inherited new segment, Order knew he would need to personally visit Party members living there. Alex Higgins was left leaning and preselection support was a sensible precaution as a middle of the road Member in case someone decided to challenge him as their new MLA who did not share the views of his predecessor.

Information about the area to the east he had lost to his next electorate, currently held by the Opposition, also needed to be passed across to the Party machine. They would have any polling booth statistics already, but local knowledge about the residents would be important to see if the Opposition's hold on the seat had been strengthened or weakened by the redistribution.

This was not always easy to guess and required on-the-ground attention. Low rent accommodation or housing for military families could be decided with reasonable accuracy, but new aged care or high-rise flats often the reason for the change proved more difficult: the former because they could have moved in from anywhere and not simply locally and the latter because affordable housing, as it had for most of the century, was out of most young people's reach. Now they were as likely as retirees to live in the high-rise with their young families, using the public playing areas for their children between the towering blocks instead of the old traditional backyards of yesteryear.

Next morning's Party meeting clarified the situation because more detailed boundary maps were available. A few mistakes, probably typo's, were picked up: a boundary line through a small shopping centre, another through a park, but these were easily rectified and most Members believed they could survive the changes.

Not so Wendy the Wonder Woman, VW for short, and Deputy Speaker.

Her seat had been abolished by carving it into sections to adjoining electorates, the majority comfortably held by the Opposition. Even the most optimistic fellow MLA knew she had no chance of winning any of the reorganised constituencies.

The sisterhood wanted to be compensated and the preselection struggles were to be renewed because there were no free seats. Members did not retire when in government and the prospect of winning again and Ministerial preference was a possibility. Even Paul Severin had had a change of heart and would be standing – or so he told colleagues and constituents.

Granted, a new seat had been created from the new suburbs to the south-east of the Territory, but its political leanings would only be known accurately following the next election result. So-called experts could and did make predictions, but these did not satisfy Wendy Wonder. She wanted blue ribbon surety, which she believed she deserved, and besides the new electorate was too far out and she had no wish to give up her comfortable, established home.

Living in the electorate was not a prerequisite. However living too far away risked criticism and seeking election from a cluster of new suburbs where people were establishing themselves, their families and their gardens with all the absence of services and infra-structure this often entailed, called for a local Member who shared their problems.

The sisterhood began a determined search to unseat a sitting member at preselection.

Among the male backbenchers nobody was safe and while Ministers were off limits the threat included Speaker Order, Govern-ment Whip Glasson, Leader of the House Harrison 'Will' Ogilvie, Graham, Higgins, Severin etc.

The most compelling argument used in favour of change was the need for more women in the Parliament, particularly against those men who didn't seem to be doing much to earn their salary.

This was a difficult matter to measure. Was constant publicity an indication of serving the community? Was a strong independent stand and threats to cross the floor and vote against your Party looking after the interests of your constituents? Was proposing contentious legislation such a George Graham's population limit for Canberra in the best interests of the ACT?

"They're moving on Finn," Rob Glasson reported to Order at one of their increasingly irregular lunches.

Order liked Finn, an inoffensive backbencher. Nevertheless he silently was relieved. The still unclear 'mutual friendship' of Wendy Wonder and Madam A could still be used to damage his preselection chances in this bitter struggle of self-interest.

"He sleeps a lot in the Chamber," Order agreed. From his vantage point it was obvious. "Will he put up a fight?"

"Doubt it. His wife's unwell."

"But it's not what they wanted for VW. It's marginal an' held I believe because he's so well liked."

"That's all she's getting, according to Bernie. Take it or leave it and if I was Wendy, I'd leave it. She's no hope."

THIRTY

Order and his staff estimated there were up to 1000 new voters in his moved boundary. One afternoon he walked through the streets with Todd, trying to judge the social class he was inheriting from Alex Higgins. Apart from identifying a couple of Party supporters his inspection was not much help and the area's voting statistics no better.

It was egalitarian middle-class suburbia, built in the 70's and 80's of the last century. Brick and brick veneer three bedroom homes of unremarkable architectural design. Front bedroom beside an unused front veranda which in turn fronted a lounge room, neat lawns and gardens occasionally shamed by an unkempt house and unmown jungle. There were such properties too numerous to count across Canberra.

The flats and units were the problem when it came to estimating population numbers. Along with dual occupancies they were creeping into the uniform street patterns and, often of modern design, stuck out like a gold tooth in an otherwise ordinary mouth.

"I've no choice," Order decided, after he agreed with Todd a pamphlet explaining the new electoral arrangements was essential. "I'll have to doorknock as well."

It was an election necessity not in as much favour as in the past with all the new technology now available for invading people's privacy. And it was a campaign tool Order disliked: if he didn't welcome uninvited visits why should other people?

"The letter won't be enough. Some of them won't read it, a few can't read it," he explained to Todd on the way back to the office. "Then there's the No Junk Mail which can offend people an' the ethnics who often don't understand."

"What if there's nobody home when you call?"

"If there's enough of those I can go back, otherwise I'll send a Dear Resident letter to the address." It was a mercy he would not have to repeat the intrusive wearying exercise, technology would take over for future voter contact.

Order also suggested a pamphlet be dropped in his lost constituency area, explaining the boundary alterations and thanking the residents for their past support.

Todd was impressed by the attention paid to the surrendered section until he was reminded adjustments occasionally were reversed due to population changes so such insurance as not wasted.

The Threeways imbroglio was shelved until closer to the election. Everyone was too busy consolidating their new gains which had a domino effect across Canberra. Order's media officer finally was earning his salary.

The Meet-the-Member evening was disappointing. Held between six and eight during the Assembly dinner break in case the House was sitting and in a Uniting Church hall in the middle of the new boundary area, it attracted twenty seven people, including three Party members and Todd. Not surprising, Order knew, because unless it was The Chief himself or a protest meeting – virtually the same thing – people were not interested, taking their democratic rights for granted.

Emmie's offer to accompany him on his doorknocking forays was welcome and although she called off subsequent weekend afternoons he thought she improved the response he received, even if they were thought initially to be Jehovah's Witnesses.

The boundary changes kept Order fully occupied with an election perhaps sooner than expected, so he didn't give another thought to

Phil Newman's resurrection until Laura reminded Emmie at their coffee club the man wanted to speak with him.

"What is it, Newman?" Order asked impatiently, stressed from a testing Question Time which almost saw the Leader of the Opposition suspended from the Chamber.

"I've been thinking," said the smooth voice after extending pleasantries, "the Plummer necklace has quite a history, quite a story. How much d'you think a magazine or a newspaper might pay?"

An' how much do you want to stay silent, Order thought, simultaneously wondering how long the curse would continue to haunt.

"Of course," Newman continued when no answer was forthcoming, "to be done properly it would have to be a comprehensive account, detailing everything, including all those involved."

"Are you in property, Newman, or really a professional blackmailer?"

"Just trying to make a dollar, John. As you're probably aware Laura is keeping me afloat at present and it's doing nothing for my self-esteem."

"So for a fat cheque you're prepared to bite the hand feeding you?"

"That would depend, John. For a consideration I'm prepared to be selective in my story telling, even if the price is right, to favourably embellish the role of people involved."

"You're disgusting, Newman."

"Perhaps, but you have a week, Order. Seven days to the auction."

"I wonder if Laura knows," Emmie said when Order told her that night.

"Unlikely. She's someone most likely to be hurt. You can bet Newman will sensationalise his story."

"If that's possible. I'll ask her."

THIRTY ONE

"Laura knows nothing about a press article, John. In fact she hotly denied Phil Newman would even stoop so low. Okay, you can shake your head in disbelief but she's in love with him! "

"I had to promise not to raise the subject again if I wanted to stay friends," Emmie continued.

"An' you gave up the chance?"

"She's lonely, John," as if that explained the feminine logic which retained a friendship Emmie didn't enjoy, "but I had her promise to say nothing to Newman about our conversation."

Laura and Emmie now continued their coffee club meetings almost exclusively in the Andrew penthouse overlooking Lake Burley Griffin because Laura believed people were staring at her in more public places.

Thus Emmie became among the first to know Harris Andrew had been admitted to hospital.

"No idea," she replied to Order's question upon his condition, "but Laura's in a panic about her own bail condition. Does she see it revoked and go back to jail for no fault of her own?"

Order agreed it did seem unfair and offered to make enquiries of The Chief, who also was Attorney-General.

"Fatima wants to speak to you too," Emmie added. "She doesn't want to be deported."

She explained the Filipino maid was worried now both of her employers were no longer actively using her services, betraying the concern Harris Andrew might not be coming back to the penthouse so she no longer had a job.

"Like so many of her people she sends money home where her mother looks after her young son."

"I don't think she will have any trouble. Laura can take over if necessary once we sort out her situation."

"That's part of the problem. Laura doesn't think it's right. Fatima's being exploited by the wicked First World."

"So we send her home to starve?"

"No, we increase Third World aid."

Reluctantly and following largely irrelevant discussion about overpopulation, Laura agreed Fatima could see John Order and place her fears before him.

"She doesn't know anyone else as important as you, John. Not even her parish priest. And she's frightened, so I've offered to come with her," Emmie confirmed.

Fatima was clearly overawed by the Speaker's office and, Order suspected, by the procedures and security to get there. All of which he hoped would give her confidence something could be done to sort out her worries.

She had dressed in her Sunday best, which probably meant she had time off too to go to church, Order noted, but Fatima was not the only visitor to make an impression.

He had not realised of the many women of his clandestine affairs, Emmie was the first ever to have visited his office and met his staff. Liz, in particular, who had spoken on the phone with her was impressed and with reason. Emmie had dressed to impress and with distinction.

The colours matched, the hair shone and the figure attracted. A poor judge of women's outfits, Order was proud of her.

They sat at the visitor's round table and Order put Fatima's concerns to rest, at least to the best of his ability.

In recent years and over the objections of egalitarian Australians, the country had allowed the poor of Asia and the Pacific the chance to work as servants and labourers in its affluent society, similar to the jobs available from years before in the oil rich Middle East.

The rules were simple and strict: no families and the duration here was of limited time. However if for some reason, unspecified to prevent abuse, the time had not expired, another job could be taken to expiration. Extension of these working visas also could be granted and were popular for people wanting to retain maids and housekeepers.

It was in the latter category Order saw Fatima with her un-blemished record of service being allowed to stay even with a new employer.

Fatima's English was passable and better than the often screeching tones employed by overseas telephone canvassers, usually Indian or Filipino, of years past before they were banned.

She was grateful to Order and explained how important a job was in Australia to her family at home. She also understood she might have to change households if Mr. Andrew did not return from hospital.

"It is so sad Mr. Andrew is sick and Mrs. Andrew fell and died." Fatima crossed herself.

"Slipped," said Order.

"No fell. Mr. Andrew tried to save her."

"Wasn't it your day off, Fatima?" Order asked. Emmie now was holding the woman's hand.

Fatima explained it was, however she had been making a cake for Father Sheehan and was running late. She was opening the downstairs door from the kitchen which allowed you across the foyer to the lounge room and to the main entrance when she saw her employers at the top of the stairs.

She was not supposed to leave by the main entrance but she was late for the bus. However she checked her movement and watched through no more than a chink in the door as Mrs. Andrew fell down the stairs screaming. Mr. Andrew watched for a moment, then came down the stairs, examined the body and went out to the lift.

"And what did you do, Fatima? " Order said gently.

"Nothing. I was scared. I knew Mrs. Andrew was dead the way she was lying. I thought Mr. Andrew had gone to get help and I need not be involved. I'm frightened of the police and I wanted to keep my job."

Frightened or not you're going to have to speak to them now, decided Order.

"Fatima, where can I contact Father Sheehan?"

THIRTY TWO

Father Sheehan was a plump bald-headed man who served the Filipino Catholic faithful in Canberra. He previously had spent time in the Philippines and spoke fluent Tagalog. His presence was a great comfort to Fatima as she answered Gabby Williams' questions, her replies noted down by Sergeant Varna, the diligent silent policewoman.

"I didn't have long," Gabby explained later. "Andrew, even with tubes and flashing lights, was conscious and clear headed. He readily admitted he pushed his wife down the stairs then claimed he found her later."

"He told me he was dying without overseas medical treatment, so perhaps it doesn't matter anymore," Order contributed.

"Doubt he'll stand trial," concluded Williams, hanging up.

We should have seen it, reasoned Order. Given the chance to get rid of the troublesome necklace with only an alcoholic wife standing in the way the temptation was too great.

On Fatima's day off he just needed to call into the penthouse between visiting his construction sites. Being seen returning home didn't matter, Grace Andrew could have fallen anytime in the space of several hours and drinking secretly in her top floor room – common behaviour among dipsomaniacs, he understood – made the deadly fall easier to organise. Only the kindly act of a Filipino maid in making a cake for her parish priest had ruined a perfect crime.

The media would headline the story if the police decided to release these new revelations. It wasn't every day you had two killers of different victims in the one family, but as Grace Andrew's fall still was regarded as an accident and her husband's healthy recovery uncertain, it might be prudent to delay going public.

For once Order was not involved in the sad business of the deaths even if his interest in the Plummer necklace resulted in a peripheral association. He was pleased this was the case. He found his new relationship with Emmie was rewarding, a gap in his life hitherto inadequately filled by electoral work had been plugged.

No more lonely meals in restaurants or predatory hunts for women for social or physical company which so often proved awkward. And no more empty weekends when it was too cold, too wet, even too hot, for campaigning now were occupied with sharing usually mundane chores and he would not again deal with the uncomfortable situation of finding someone – or not –to accompany him to functions. Bliss!

* * *

Still sorting out initiatives to further connect with his new voters, Order did not notice a week had elapsed since Newman's unsettling telephone conversation and only was reminded when the man phoned.

"I haven't had time – " began Order, hoping to forestall whatever threat was coming.

"You've a stay of execution, John," interrupted Newman. "Somethings come up I need to address first before I approach the media, but I can assure you the story will be bigger for the delay."

"So how long this time?" Order realised there was nothing he could pay to prevent the story breaking, but if he had notice he might be able to be prepared.

"I'll give you warning," promised Newman and rang off.

"What an odious character," Emmie declared when she was told. "No consideration for Laura or her sick father."

"And maybe that's the problem!" Order exclaimed. "Harris Andrew's in hospital, ill. Newman doesn't want to act on the story until he either recovers or dies. It wouldn't be a good look exposing a sick man."

"More likely he hopes he can get more money from Laura to hush things up if Mr. Andrew dies," Emmie said accurately. "The estate that is."

Intrigued by Newman's promise the story would be bigger for the delay, Order contacted Gabby Williams the next morning and had the big man's answer that afternoon when the policeman visited his office.

"Phil Newman knows Andrew killed his wife, just as you suspected," he confirmed.

"Therefore the story is bigger for the delay should Andrew die or recover. The exposure would really add zero's to the media payment."

"He told Newman about the murder to explain how he could now get rid of the necklace without his wife objecting."

Unguarded moment but dumb, thought Order. However Newman doesn't know the police are aware of the murder through Fatima, the maid, and Harris Andrew had been asked by Gabby to keep the confession to himself.

"I suggested it would save his daughter pain. They've reconciled and she visits. He agreed."

Harris Andrew died two days later.

THIRTY THREE

Despite an upbringing in the squalor of a sectarian-divided Pyrmont, Harris Andrew was not a religious man and the funeral was held at the South Canberra crematorium beyond Tuggeranong.

Order elected not to attend. Apart from an intimate circle his dealings with the late developer were unknown and he saw no reason to expose the ignorance. Emmie was another matter. Laura asked her to accompany her to the service, Phil Newman being, perhaps conveniently, out of town.

"Lots of men from the industry, I think," Emmie reported back to him. "Builders and such looking uncomfortable in suits and ties."

"Not many women," she continued, trying to retain his attention. "Wives, I suppose, but I tracked down the girlfriend. Laura recognised her from the penthouse visit. Name's Iris."

The name was familiar, then he remembered his visit to Andrew at his construction site. He hadn't seen her but Iris was the name of the man's secretary. An all-too-regular third party in matrimonial threesomes.

If Order was inattentive it was with good reason: a strong rumour suggested an election within the next three months.

The Opposition's internecine warfare over their leadership had escalated almost into public mutiny and they were in no position to go to the polls. The Chief also was aware all was not peaceful in the government's ranks: the new electoral boundaries and the sisterhood's push for more female candidates had led to dissatisfaction. The prospect of an imminent election would concentrate the minds and efforts of the dissatisfied on more important matters: their own political futures.

A spin-off as Order reminded Rob Glasson was the future of the Assembly's dining room probably would not be decided before the Parliament was prorogued and who knew what the composition of the new parliament would be? With committees' scrambling to complete inquiries before the House rose neither MLA could see this select committee's reference having priority.

"The backbenchers are all busy on other referrals, they're too time-poor making up quorums on everything," Glasson pointed out, acknowledging a favourite government ploy to keep restless Members occupied. "And they need time to campaign."

As did Order, so he was pleased any distractions like the Plummer necklace had been largely removed. Largely but not entirely, because he waited impatiently for Phil Newman to contact him again.

He hoped the man would not reach any media agreements before he settled with Order, but suspected his greed would encourage him to seek the easier money first.

Nevertheless he was shocked when Newman did phone him.

"One hundred thousand!"

"You politicians are overpaid. You can afford it and think of how deeply I could – only could, mind you – have you involved and perhaps an election in the offing?" the smooth voice argued threateningly.

"I'll need more time."

"Until Friday, Order. Take out a loan, your credit is good, I'm sure, Mr. Speaker, and I'll take a bank cheque."

"How can I trust you?"

"You can't. Just my word. Now, when and where do we meet?"

Because the Assembly was not sitting Order arranged for the

payment to be made 10.30 am Friday morning, time for him to visit the bank and arrange matters before the meeting.

A smug Phil Newman, tieless but neatly dressed, was shown back into the office he had visited months ago.

"Close the door, please Liz."

Order ushered Newman to the visitor's round table where Emmie already was sitting. His attention however was directed to the office door which opened again almost immediately.

"Phil, you've met Detective Inspector Williams and Sergeant Shanks before, I believe?" as the two policemen entered the room.

"What's all this about, Order?" It was almost a snarl, not so much of anger but of outrage at being caught out.

"Blackmail," said Williams.

Newman relaxed, the snarl replaced with a confident smirk.

"Prove it," he said.

"We will if we have to, but you're also faced with concealing a crime. Murder."

"If you're talking about say, Harris Andrew, he's dead."

"But not before we obtained a taped confession and a statutory declaration wherein the deceased confirms he told you he killed his wife, Grace Wilde Andrew, and why he did it."

Order was not sure listening to Williams which irritated him most: the stilted jargon of the charge or the use of the American second name now a feature of women's nomenclature.

"He's still dead, "said Newman, but with less confidence Order thought. "If I deny the whole story as the ravings of a sick man browbeaten by you police, there's no way he can correct me."

"There's his daughter – " began Williams.

"She knows nothing. Anyway, she's in love with me an' will do anything I say, poor fool. So no problem." Confidence had returned.

"True," interposed Order when Gabby Williams' looked un-comfortable, "but this will make great extra copy for your media revelations, except you won't come out of it as well as you expected."

"With charges pending about concealing a crime," Williams added, re-joining the fray. "And I'm not sure we couldn't impound your media payment under the proceeds of crime legislation, as well."

"You'll get nothing, Newman," Order said gleefully as the office door opened again and Laura entered followed by Liz.

"My phone was on broadcast," Order announced after a nod from his secretary.

Before Sergeant Shanks could stop her, a weeping Laura walked across to her lover and delivered a stinging slap to Newman's face.

"Enough!" said Williams, as Emmie took the sobbing woman in her arms. "Take Mr. Newman to the station, Sergeant, we need a statement."

"Perhaps you'd like to go the back way, Phil? " Order offered magnanimously. "This time of day our front entrance is swarming with inquisitive reporters and TV crews. Liz will show the way an' collect your pass after you leave the building."

THIRTY FOUR

"She's in the Remand Centre," Emmie responded to his question. "There was nobody left to take care of her."

"No, I couldn't, wouldn't," she added, "and I don't know if it would be legally possible."

Best not anyway. They had been kept out of the mess so far, why get involved now with a possible election soon? Instead he asked if any date had been set for the trial.

"If you mean Laura's, no, and if you mean Newman's, I don't know. There might not be one, but I'm not game to ask her anything about him in case she gets upset."

"What about her father's company?"

"Selling it, but given her situation it's very complicated."

"I suppose the Public Trustee will have to administer her affairs and the money until she comes out."

"If she goes in," Emmie said for both of them.

And there the issue of Laura's future rested. Emmie continued to visit her regularly and reported she appeared in good health but often vague.

For Order the redistribution changing the electoral boundaries took up much of his time and that of his staff. It was an irony Todd, his underused media officer, now found more than enough to do planning promotional activities in the new section of the electorate.

However several weeks later Harris Andrew's published probate notice took him back to the complications of the Plummer necklace and what looked to be an even greater issue of the late developer's construction empire.

Could Laura inherit the sale money going to jail and if so, what would she do with it? Would her dream of using it for her green projects be unusually realised? What about the Assembly committee's inquiry, was it now closed down? What about Andrew's girlfriend, Iris? Would she be a beneficiary in the estate? Finally, what about Phil Newman?

Laura's situation intrigued him and Order was interested what had happened to Fatima. Was there to be another inquest? If so, she would need to attend and did she have another job? Gabby Williams would know.

"Gone," said Sergeant Shanks.

"Gone where?" Very unlike Gabby Williams.

"He's retired, Mr. Order."

"I don't understand," Order admitted.

"Well, Mr. Williams was not one to make a fuss –" Shanks began.

"Where has he gone?"

"Down the coast, up to Queensland. Wherever. It's for fishing."

And Order realised he knew nothing about the man, only as a policeman, which would always be the situation.

"He'll be back for the trial?"

"Yes," said Shanks but doubtfully, leaving Order wondering which trial he meant and if he meant the proceedings itself or the role of his ex-boss in it.

Order realised the Plummer necklace and its alleged curse had broken more than a few lives, it had indirectly severed a personal and indispensable link he enjoyed with the local police. It would never be the same again, his amateur sleuthing days were over.

Emmie could not conceal her delight, while he wondered aloud if the curse did exist would it continue its malevolent effect upon the new owner.

"What happened to the necklace in Hong Kong?" he asked.

"I questioned Laura about that months ago and she said once it was identified as almost worthless paste they swapped it for a ring – since mislaid – and the merchant said he'd break it up to sell as cheap jewellery."

Leaving Order to wonder if the curse was as strong in the sum of its parts in the broken up Plummer necklace.

THE END